In the rapids

NEW SOUTH AFRICAN STORIES

Compiled by
Linda Rode and Jakes Gerwel

KWELA BOOKS

Cover design by Konrad Rode
Book design by Nazli Jacobs
Set in Plantin
Printed and bound by NBD
Drukkery Street, Goodwood, Western Cape
First edition, first printing 2001

ISBN 0-7957-0125-X

Acknowledgements

Stories originally written in Afrikaans were
translated by Maren Bodenstein.
"The immortality of lobsters" was translated
by the author, Tom Dreyer, and
"Compress" by Chris van Wyk.

This collection is also available in Afrikaans
as *Stroomversnelling*.

Contents

Foreword

In 1995 Kwela published its first book: *Crossing over*, a collection of new "stories for a new South Africa". With *In the rapids* the aim we had set ourselves in putting together *Crossing over* has once again been reached to a happy degree. It is heartening that this follow-up collection of thirty new stories, like its predecessor, displays contributions from widely divergent cultural and linguistic backgrounds, and that the work of established as well as of a significant number of new authors could be included. To make the stories accessible to a wider reading public, contributions originally written in Afrikaans have been translated into English for *In the rapids*, and vice versa for the Afrikaans version, *Stroomversnelling*.

The spectrum of voices audible in *In the rapids* surprises the reader with on the one hand, the staggering variety of themes, and with striking similarities in the depiction of the human condition on the other. The collection exudes a distinct tonality: All the stories (also those which deal with past events) are constructed around the experiences of young people. These include a redemptive experience which restores the voice of a girl who had stopped speaking (Marita van der Vyver); the mystery of early, only half-understood experiences (Jeanne Goosen); the realisation of the true essence of being a good Samaritan (George Weideman); the short-lived consolation of a physical encounter (Arja Salafranca); how the regional pronunciation of a single word becomes a key to unlocking a criminal secret (E.K.M. Dido); loneliness and outsidership (Felicity Wood); violence that penetrates even the most secret spaces of the body and soul (Melvin Whitebooi, Marcel Williams); childhood fear (Rrekgetsi Chimeloane); the hampering effect of stereotyping (Buntu Siwisa); liberation (Elsa Joubert, Bridget Pitt); homecoming (Diana Ferrus); boisterous humour (Jenny Hobbs); a mini thriller (François Bloemhof).

It is notable that a large number of contributions is in the first person. In this collection the gaze often turns inwards. Although first-person narration is a well-known stylistic device to ensure immediacy, its striking use in this collection may signify something more – an attempt to come closer, to reach out to others. A subtle, probably unconscious emphasis of the fact that if there is an "I", it automatically implies a "you". Getting under the skin of others is one of the possibilities that this collection offers readers.

The phenomenon of so many of the stories being told in the first person has also had a side-effect: colourful and distinctive words and phrases from a specific setting have been incorporated unchanged and in the original language. Each of these stories presents a particular voice, and we wanted to retain its unique character and intimacy. Words which may be unfamiliar are explained in the word list on page 162.

As with *Crossing over*, readers of all ages will be able to relate to these stories; the reality that is depicted is not unknown. What takes one by surprise, and sometimes even throws one off guard, is the individuality of the different voices.

The compilers
Cape Town, July 2001

Arja Salafranca

Sour milk, cold ash

JUDE HAS RINGLETS OF DYED BLONDE HAIR and big, sloping eyes rimmed in fashionable black eyeliner. Her long, lean body is sheathed in a peach skintight dress.

She has these looks she uses to catch men. She's not using them now, while talking to her friend Dale, but soon she'll lower her head, drop her eyes demurely, and catch another one. It's so easy.

"You've got to hurt them," she tells Dale, fingering her friend's fine blonde hair. "Look at this," she says, "look at this power, this beauty. You could kill men with this." She draws hard on a cigarette.

It's Saturday night. There are only a couple of locals in The Wild Monkey, a club which is anything but wild, in a neighbourhood without much of a nightlife. The pub will probably close down soon.

A band is screeching out a rhythm to which some are trying to dance.

For now Jude and Dale are sitting there, watching the evening go by.

Jude stops talking, and she shouts their order to the bartender. "This place is so dull," she says, rolling her eyes.

Dale agrees, pouring some cider down her throat, as if she hopes that will get her in the mood. She stares at the deserted dance floor.

"We'll get pissed," Jude decides. "We'll get so pissed we won't know where we are."

It seems like a good plan. Since they won't be going anywhere else fast, anyway. Both eighteen, they still don't have driver's licences. Sometimes they get a ride with other friends, but it didn't work out tonight. So here they are, watching the evening dissolve in waiting.

Then Jude gets up, high on rum and coke. She stands in the middle of the dance floor in the skintight dress that hugs her body and reaches down to her ankles. Dancing on her own, she is spotlighted.

Dale watches. Men's eyes stare hungrily at Jude, taking in the body beneath the dress.

11

Jude dances slowly, curving her body around the cacophony of sounds, dancing slower and slower as the pace hots up. She can feel those eyes on her; the rum has made her head spin around. She walks back to the counter, where Dale is talking to a group of people who have just walked in, people Jude doesn't know. Jude forgets their names after the introductions have been made. She orders another drink.

Jude wanders off. Dale's involved in her conversation. She won't miss her.

She walks into the toilet. The harsh fluorescent glow makes her skin look alabaster, her eyes stand out hollow and empty. She smears shadow around them, picks at her lashes, coated thickly in mascara, smacks her lips in red.

There's a rattle floating in one of the toilets. Jude wonders how it got there.

A girl is swallowing some pills by the basins. Jude watches as her throat moves once, twice, three times with every pill. The girl catches her eye, doesn't even smile as she swallows again. Her eyes are dead.

The band is packing up. Dale's been looking for her. "Listen, we're all going to Club Ashtray, John's got his dad's minibus, they can give us a lift. Let's go. There's nothing happening here."

Jude nods.

It's one in the morning as they drive through slumbering suburbia. She notices Dale talking to her friends. Jude doesn't like them much. They seem so stiff, so proper, so earnest. But she doesn't care. They've got a ride, that's what counts. She digs out comps for Club Ashtray. She has piles of them, each time she goes they give her more. She'll never use them all. She looks at Dale, suddenly grateful to her for knowing all these people.

Club Ashtray is packed as usual. Jude gets onto the dance floor and ignores the group. Now and again she smiles to let everyone know she's there. It seems to reassure them. The music is loud, hard, pumping, it's good. They're playing all her favourite songs. Dale shouts in her ear that they're going onto the outside balcony. Jude follows, distanced by a drink someone put in her hand, distanced by her want.

"I've done it in alleyways, in garden sheds, in a bakkie, in some guy's bed high on speed, and in a room with Led Zeppelin on the walls and Metallica playing," she told Dale once.

Dale had just looked at her, then asked when she had first had sex.

"Fourteen," Jude told her. "It was over so quickly. And it was sore."

Now she is watching Dale, wondering why they are friends. Dale seems so much happier with these other people around her. She's almost disregarding her, although she has tried now and again to include Jude in the conversation. Dale's friends are so normal, it's boring, Jude decides, leaning her head against the railing. The night air is cold, the bars are hard. Conversations are starting and stopping around her. Others are silent, listening to the music, or high on something.

"Don't you ever worry about getting pregnant? Or getting Aids?" Dale had often asked when they first met.

"No. I know it's stupid. But I just can't help it. Sometimes the guy's got a condom. But mostly not. I don't know. I just never fall pregnant."

She didn't worry about Aids. She didn't think she'd ever get it. And if she did, let her parents deal with that.

Dale flicks her hair back, speaking to one of the guys in the group. She's wearing her usual pair of jeans. Suddenly, Jude wants to get up and shout at Dale, asking her why for once in her life she doesn't wear something more sexy, a low top, shorts, a dress, anything. But Dale doesn't dress like that. She could stuff men up if she wanted. Stuff them up and leave them, till they wanted more and she wouldn't give it.

Jude goes back onto the dance floor. Her body aches as she scans the place.

She stands back for a while, watching, drinking rum, feeling it melt through her. A guy taps her on the shoulder, smiling. She smiles back. She thinks she met him two weeks ago. She had been with a friend of his, and vaguely remembers being introduced to him. But she cannot remember his name.

"Do you remember me?" he asks.

"Of course," she says. He gets her a drink, asks her to dance.

Jude asks where his friend is tonight. The guy just shrugs. He must be somewhere else. She dances with him, discovers his name is Jack.

He slips his arm around her. Soon they are colliding as they move together. His breath is hot above her ears, she can feel him breathing, his chest against her, firm and strong. It is hot in the club, and the bodies are sandwiched onto the dance floor. Sweat is pouring down the front of her dress and her face, making her forehead prickle. He's sweating too. A slightly meaty smell.

He forces his tongue into her mouth. That familiar rubbery sensation of tongue against tongue, Jude's head stretches back as they kiss and dance. His hand circles her buttocks, she slips hers around his, but feels nothing through the solid denim.

Chest to chest, she feels his shirt is soaked with sweat. Her dress is also wet. He keeps on probing with his tongue and hands. Jude's head is far, far away from her body, almost as though she is watching herself from above. But that's never happened. She always manages to stay inside her body. She wishes he'd do something.

Eventually he leads her away from the grind of the dance floor. "Come home with me," he hisses into her ear. She shakes her head. Dale is still somewhere around, and will miss her.

"My flat's just around the corner, I promise." She looks for Dale, decides to take a chance as she can't see her anywhere.

Running through the cool night air, she finds he did tell her the truth. He lives around the corner. Through a deserted alley, to the front door of the derelict building. In darkness they clatter through the silence up the staircase.

Jack is serious now. When he flings open the door, the dirty yellow bulbs illuminate the mattress on the floor. The Formica-topped table is surrounded by chairs, the sink is spilling over with dishes, the milk stands soured on the counter.

It's over quickly. As usual. A speedy shooting off of clothes, those first few moments exploring bodies, when he comments on her perfect body, how beautiful she is. Those things mean nothing. It's just a way of trying. They need not bother to make her feel good. This is when they have her where they want her, this is what she's aimed for the entire evening. This familiar fleeting warmth.

Afterwards, they lie on his mattress.

He offers her coffee, if she wants. She refuses – the milk is off, anyway.

The journey back is less exhilarating. This time she's cold, and the clinging sweat makes her even colder. When she shivers, Jack just looks at her.

Back in the pulsating hot club, she's still cold. Jack asks the bartender for paper, writes down her number, says he'll call soon. Perhaps he will. She nods numbly as Dale comes toward her. They're leaving now.

She kisses Jack goodbye. Dale hadn't even missed her. Well, it had been better than she expected. It was always more comfortable doing it on a bed.

She knows she wants more than this. She would like these men to tell her she has a beautiful body because they love her or think she's special. But for now, there is only this. The quickness that fills up the loneliness and hunger, the great yawning emptiness inside her. The fear of waking up to yet another day, the sunshine crushing into your face, to a house where her aged parents are sleeping, getting even older.

"Who was that guy you were with?" Dale asks.
    "Jack. I met him through a friend. He kisses well."
    "Are you going to see him again?"
    "Maybe ... if he calls."

MARITA VAN DER VYVER

She doesn't speak

"HER NAME IS ANOUK AND SHE DOESN'T SPEAK."

That is how my mother always introduces me to other people.

My name is Noekie, I always say without moving my lips or making a sound. I speak all the time in my head, to myself.

If anybody wants to know more about it she would say: "No, she isn't dumb." Almost casually, as if there was nothing strange about a four-teen-year-old who doesn't speak. "She stopped speaking after experiencing a traumatic incident."

Usually people don't ask any more questions after that. At least not immediately. Usually they would be scared off by the words *traumatic incident*. But later, if they wanted to know more, she would tell them everything. Like a tap that had been opened, the words would just pour from her – how the robbers burst into our lounge one evening and shot my father dead and how she was seriously wounded and how I saw it all while I was hiding behind the kitchen door with the maid, Rebecca. How Rebecca had pushed me behind the door and had held her hand over my mouth while Dad's blood stained the Persian carpet. How she had tried to crawl to her handbag to get to her cell phone while the robbers were searching the bedroom for money or jewels or whatever they were looking for. How she pretended to be dead when they came back into the lounge.

Do you see what I mean? I don't need to speak. My mother speaks enough for both of us.

The robbers had hardly looked at her. They had run out through the verandah door when they saw a car with a blue light patrolling the street. It was a security company's car, a routine patrol, like there was every evening. But the robbers probably didn't know about this. They had probably thought that one of the neighbours had heard suspicious sounds. Usual-ly when my mother gets to this part of the story she gives a dejected

16

little laugh: "Even if someone had suspected something," she would add, "they wouldn't have been able to see anything from the street. A few months before, my husband had built a high wall around the property to protect us."

My mother believes that the more you talk about a difficult thing the easier it will be to bear – my mother and all the psychologists I have already seen. But as yet, no one has been able to tell me about what you should do when something is so difficult that you simply can't talk about it. In the beginning I really tried. Forcing the sounds out of my throat like dry vomit. They said that if I forced myself to speak about it I would stop dreaming about it. But after a few awful sessions with a psychologist the nightmares just got worse.

"It was Rebecca who dialled the emergency number and got the ambulance to come. Saved my life. And Anouk's. If the child had made a single sound ..."

What my mother doesn't say is that maybe we could have saved my father's life too. Maybe if I had slipped out the back door and called the neighbours, if I had stayed calm and done something. If I had just acted like Buffy against the vampires or someone like that. But I went rigid, scared stiff. Mute.

"And that is why we are living in England now."

That is how my mother always ends her story. As if the attack was the only reason why we had left. She doesn't say that she had wanted to go and live in England long before the attack. Her father was British and she had the right passport. She had always stood with one foot in the sea, ready to emigrate, every time she read a newspaper heading that scared her. It was my father who didn't want to go. He loved his country. So did I.

"I'm not going anywhere," Dad had said in his quiet way. "Over my dead body."

Then he died. And then we left.

It's almost three years since we moved. We live in a quiet village east of London where everything is so green that after a while you start longing for something pale and dry to look at. Brown soil that has been baked dry, this is what I miss. Soil that burns your feet, like on my father's family farm in the Free State. Pale veld and a cloudless sky and the taste of dust.

My mother doesn't miss anything. At least that is what she says. She didn't even want to come back on a holiday. I think she is scared to see all the things she misses. But now we are here on holiday – because she thinks it will be good for me. She wants to see me laugh again. But we have been back for a week already and I still haven't seen anything that makes me want to laugh.

"Doesn't she want to talk?" asks one of my mother's friends. She wears far too much make-up. All my mother's old friends from Pretoria wear far too much make-up. But this one's neck almost snaps from all the mascara. "Or is it that she can't talk?"

I am sitting on the other side of the same room, reading. People seem to think that if you can't speak you also can't hear. After a while they don't see you any more. I have become used to being treated like a piece of furniture. At school too, the kids talk right over my head, look right past me as if I am not there.

"It's probably a combination of factors," my mother replies, giving her what-did-I-do-to-deserve-such-a-daughter sigh. "At first she couldn't speak and then she didn't want to any more, and now … who knows?"

"Doesn't she know how lucky she is to be living in England!" Lashes heavy with mascara flutter and she utters a forced little laugh. "I wish I could leave this country!"

"Anouk won't be happy anywhere," my mother says after another long drawn-out sigh. "Not until she has worked through the past."

Work through the past. A combination of factors. A traumatic experience. My mother uses words like bricks to build walls around her, to protect herself. As if she doesn't know that walls cannot protect one.

Anouk is another one of her bricks. Anouk isn't me, Anouk is someone exotic, worldly, my mother's dream daughter with long dark hair. I am not exotic. I am small and ordinary. My hair is short and my face bare. I wear boy's clothes and like to walk barefoot even in England where no one does that. People generally think that I am two years younger than my real age. I can't help it, I don't look like someone called Anouk, and I don't feel like someone called Anouk.

"And the psychologists?" asks my mother's friend. "Couldn't they help?"

No, Mrs Mascara, the psychologists couldn't help. After a while I refused to go, refused to try and vomit out words. And once everybody started to leave me alone I also had fewer nightmares.

They weren't less terrible, just less frequent. When they do come at night it is still as unbearable as ever. Blood on the carpet, a carpet that stains darker and darker, blood that flows over everything, furniture and walls, like brown-red paint, blood that streams out of the front door and runs down the street. Streets of blood, rivers of blood, a country full of blood. Then I also make strange noises in my sleep, my mother says, gargling, rattling noises like words in a language that doesn't exist. Sometimes I sob loudly and then my mother shakes me softly, waking me up and holding me. Sometimes she cries with me.

I loved my father. My mother probably too. I don't know. Nowadays she is going out with another man. Dad was tall and thin with a soft voice. My mother's new friend is short and stocky (well, actually he is quite fat, but my mother describes him as short and stocky). He likes to laugh loudly. He tries terribly hard to be nice to me. It's probably quite difficult to be nice to someone like me.

I wish I were someone else. No, I wish I was myself, three years ago when Dad was still alive and we still lived in Pretoria and I could stand barefoot in the kitchen in the afternoon and watch Rebecca iron the washing. I wish I could turn back the clock, be eleven years old again, and listen to the hissing of the steam iron while I make myself a peanut butter sandwich. For ever and ever.

And now my mother has this stupid idea that she wants to go and look at our old house – or rather at the wall around the house, because that is all that you can see from the street. She has brought along my Granny Anna to give her "psychological support". Support to look at a wall?

"I have forgotten how dry the Highveld gets in winter," my mother says as we drive past the Voortrekker Monument. "Or maybe it just looks paler because we have become used to a place that is always green."

Because it always rains. Because the sun never shines properly, not like it shines here in Africa.

"The grass on the other side is always greener," mumbles Granny Anna.

Not for me. I miss the pale grass on this side of the fence.

I am sitting in the back of the car, staring at the high, pale blue sky, drinking in the air as if it were water. When last did I see such a wide cloudless sky? The closer we get to our old suburb, the slower Mom drives. And the faster she talks, almost without breathing, her fingers clutching onto the steering wheel.

"Just look at all those fences! The burglar bars and the security gates! The alarm systems and the vicious dogs behind the gates! I'm sure it wasn't so bad here three years ago."

"Three years ago you just didn't notice it because you were used to it," Granny says. "Familiarity breeds contempt."

Dad always used to say that Granny Anna had swallowed a book of idioms when she was small. I sometimes wonder if she has any of her own words left in her head.

"Three years ago I didn't feel contempt, Mom. I thought it was normal to live like this. Now I live in a village where no one hides behind security gates. Where the dogs sound friendly when they bark."

"Maybe their bite is worse than their bark," Granny says with a dry laugh.

My mother doesn't catch the joke. She doesn't even listen to what Granny is saying. She is far too worked up.

"I never want to live here again!"

"What you sow you shall reap," mumbles Granny.

Mother glares at her, irritated.

"I didn't sow the crime in this country, Mom."

"The sins of the fathers …"

I had never noticed before how much they look alike from the back. Both have short, dark and smooth hair, small ears and thin necks. Their voices also sound quite similar. They say that I also look like my mother. It's hard to believe because she always wears dark red lipstick and black kohl around her eyes, which makes her look, well, quite exotic.

I can't remember what my voice sounds like. I was never much of a chatterbox anyhow. My mother was always the talker in the house and my father and I understood each other without having to say anything – Dad, me and Rebecca.

When I was small I asked many questions but when I was about seven I noticed that I could get more answers from books than from people. And so I started reading more and more and spoke less and less.

"Do you know what it's like to live in a country where you don't have to be scared all the time?"

"I refuse to live in fear, Anneke. The only thing to fear is fear itself."

As we turn into our old road my mother breathes in sharply. I remember the trees, many of them now pale and naked, but in summer they form a green canopy over the pavement. How I used to jump from shade to shade on my way to the café, barefoot, trying not to get my feet burnt by the cement. My heels were almost as rough as Becca's. My mother had bought me a grey stone to scrape my feet soft at night in the bath, but I never used it. I wanted to have feet like Becca's, soles that don't hurt on the cement, heels that can step on pieces of glass and thorns.

We stop in front of the house, the one on the left-hand side, on the corner. We stare at the high white wall and the red signs of two different security companies. The black steel gate that opens with a remote from inside the house. The driveway gate which also opens with a remote. My mother's shoulders are shaking. She is crying. My gran takes her hand, turns around and gives me a worried smile. As if concerned that I too will start crying.

I get out of the car. I am hot and I don't want to watch my mother cry because I can't bear the expression in Gran's eyes – as if she has forgiven me everything, will always love me, even if I never say another word.

I stumble across the pavement, all along the white wall, around the corner where they can't see me. My eyes are filled with tears, my ears are filled with the familiar sounds of the street, the sound of a lawn mower and the soft hum of the pool cleaners and the barking of the dogs behind the gates – not friendly dogs, not here. Voices from the radios in the kitchens, usually Zulu or Sesotho, sometimes English or Afrikaans. Screaming sirens in the distance, in another suburb, on the highway. I had forgotten about all the sirens.

On the farthest side of the property there is a smaller iron gate that Rebecca used to get to her outside room. I hold onto the gate and press my face against the bars as if I want to press right through this barrier. I look at the kitchen window, the back door and the washing line full of baby clothes. Little white vests and pink jackets. I didn't know that the new people had a baby. I wonder if they know that my father was shot dead in their lounge. It's probably not the type of thing that an estate agent tells you when she wants to sell a house.

The back door opens and my heart breaks into tiny pieces as I see Rebecca walking towards the washing line. Impossible. But it is Becca's thin black body. Becca's tough feet in her slops. Becca's familiar light pink overall. It can't be. Becca doesn't work here any more. My mother helped her to find other work before we went to England. We had sent her postcards the first year and then … we had lost contact. Someone had let us know that she no longer worked at the same address.

And now she is here standing at the washing line, of course it is she, the woman who looked after me when I was a baby. The body that I know better than my mother's, busy packing the clothes of a stranger's baby into a plastic basket.

I shake the gate to get her attention. It has to be her. But she is too far to hear anything.

"Rebeccaaa!" The voice that bursts out of my throat frightens me. It doesn't sound human. More like a dying animal, a cow bellowing, or something like that. The woman turns around, comes closer, uncertain.

"Becca?" I try again. A hoarse rattle. Once when my dad had laryngitis it sounded like that. "Is it you?"

"Noekie?" her face bursts open with joy. She drops the basket with the baby clothes onto the lawn and comes running towards the gate. Pushes her rough hands through the bars, cups my face in her hands, laughs in amazement. "Noekie! It's you!"

I laugh and cry at the same time. She takes a bunch of keys out of the pocket of her pink overall and unlocks the gate. Her hands are shaking. She pulls me close to her and presses me against her. I didn't know how much I had missed this body, the smell of clean washing and spices and ... potatoes? Nobody in England smells like this. No one in the whole world smells like this.

"Anouk?" my mother calls as she appears around the corner. "Anouk? *Rebecca*?"

"It's me, Madam." She wants to let go of me but I cling to her. "The child is very happy to see me."

"But ... what are you ... are you working here again?"

My mother's voice is high with profound surprise, her face overwhelmed. My gran stands behind her, her mouth wide open.

"Things didn't go well with the other people, Madam." Rebecca sounds embarrassed, like when she had burnt some food, as if she is scared that Mom will be cross. "And then I heard that these people were having a baby and they were looking for someone to help them. I missed having a child in the house ..."

My mother hugs Rebecca, but all the time she is looking at me, at my tear-stained face and at my laughing mouth.

"Do they treat you well?" Granny wants to know from Rebecca.

"Very good, Madam. And the little one is so cute. She reminds me a lot of Noekie when she was a baby. Also has such round, curious eyes. She will probably ask just as many questions when she begins to talk."

I laugh, a breathy rattle, and my mother's hand flies to her mouth.

"Anouk has stopped talking." Her dark red lipstick is slightly smudged, her eyes hidden behind her sunglasses. "She has stopped laughing. I thought ..."

22

"She spoke to me," Becca says proudly, teasingly, as if my mother has just made a joke. "She screamed like a mad one when she saw me."

"Anouk?"

"My name is Noekie," I say in my strange new voice. A bit less hoarse with each word. For the first time in four years it is my mother who is speechless. She stares at me, the tears dripping from under her sunglasses.

"You know I don't like to be called *Anouk*."

And with every word that comes out of my mouth I sound more like my mother.

GAVIN KRUGER

Red herrings

A LITTLE GIRL WAS FIRST TO SPOT the blond young man climbing up the side of the gleaming skyscraper.

"Look, Mom," she shrilled, "there's a man sailing up that building!"

While the mother stopped and stared, a crowd soon gathered to blare out their fears and judgements.

"Rather silly and irresponsible!"

"We should phone the police!"

"And an ambulance!"

A smartly-dressed businessman got onto his cell phone.

For a moment the climber appeared pasted down on the wall like a gingerbread man. The crowd held its breath. Then the man moved his legs, breaking the spell. Below the crowd inhaled together, as if sharing one giant lung.

The climber appeared unruffled and continued his slow ascent.

First his hands inched up, then he heaved his body along, higher up. A hand loosened suddenly and, for a moment, his body dangled precariously. But the collective gasp from the crowd seemed to will the climber along – clutching firmly to the wall, he moved on.

A little further, a disposal truck suddenly grunted with a change of gears, while being fed garbage by unconcerned workers. Angry eyes swung towards them as if to say, "Hush, don't you realise a drama is unfolding?"

"Do you think he's suicidal?"

"You bet! Only a madman would try that stunt!"

"Maybe he was ditched by a girlfriend."

"Maybe a victim of affirmative action. There are no jobs for young whites!"

"Oh, nonsense. Maybe he's just proving something to himself."

"I still say he's on a suicide mission!"

"Why all the hard work before killing himself? He could've taken the lift!"

"Who knows? Maybe he's high on drugs. The kids of today!"

"Probably Ecstacy – gives you a lift, you know?"

An arm followed by the opposite leg like a gecko climbing a window. His muscular calves, knotted like gnarled trunks, dug into the seemingly sheer wall while his ropey arms glistened with perspiration.

"He's got nice legs!"

"Just like a woman! The young man's in desperate trouble and you're licking your lips!"

A Southeaster stirred on the pavement and swirled up in gusts, rattling the window panes. The climber stayed rooted to the spot as his clothing tented and flapped about him. A momentary anxious downward glance sent a ripple of alarm through the crowd. But then a reassuring thumbs-up followed.

The crowd relished the moment, the young man's first recognition of their presence.

Just then another shrill voice pierced the air. "Help! He's snatched my bag!"

A young thief was haring down the street; bystanders looked around, willing somebody else to give chase. But there was no response.

"My bag, he's got my bag! Will somebody help me?"

When a police car appeared from nowhere, a man led the aggrieved lady to the law-enforcers before hastily resuming his place amongst the crowd. Relieved that this interruption had been taken care of, the crowd refocused their attention on the climber.

He was now only about ten metres from the top.

"I still think this is a publicity stunt – one never knows what these advertising cranks will come up with."

"No! Things have become too much for him – a new South Africa, a new millennium, the crime wave, the recession – no wonder he can't face the future!"

"Why don't you join the chicken run, my man?"

"Humph! I was born here and I'll be buried here. But it's so easy for you people now. The gravy-train has become all black – no room for anybody else!"

"You didn't complain when it was all-white!"

A shoving match started while the crowd pushed the two adversaries out of the way.

"Don't you point at me!"

"Do you hate a black finger in your face, my man?"

It was the little girl who pointed towards the climber. "See, he's on top!" She was jumping up and down clapping her hands.

The climber was unfolding something white.

"A suicide note!"

"A message to the one who'd jilted him!"

"Watch out, he's going to jump!"

A fire engine roared to a stop as firemen tumbled down. An ambulance's red light pulsed a red alert as it raced closer.

The banner in the climber's hands unfolded slowly.

"What does it say?"

People squinted while shading their eyes against the glare of the sun.

The climber held the banner aloft triumphantly.

ONE CAN STILL GET TO THE TOP
IN THE NEW SOUTH AFRICA.

Applause rippled through the crowd, but some felt cheated. Onlookers started drifting away as the two adversaries made peace and shook hands. Policemen raced into the building as the climber disappeared from sight.

The child tugged at her mother's dress. "Where's the man gone to?"

"Who knows? I hope he gets away."

"Why?"

"He ... he's done something bad, love."

"Climbing to the top?"

"Yes, he wasn't supposed to do that."

"Would it be okay if he only went halfway up?"

"No, public buildings aren't meant to be climbed!"

"Then why did the people clap their hands?"

"His banner said something nice."

"Like what?"

"Something like there's hope for all of us in our country."

She nodded, satisfied. "And that's good, isn't it, Mommy?"

When her mother nodded she screwed up her face. "Not like that naughty man who ran off with the lady's bag."

"No, that was a real scoundrel!"

"Why did everybody let him go then?" she asked, frowning. Then she pointed towards the entrance of the building where policemen were frog-marching the young man towards their vehicle. "What are they doing?" she cried out.

"Let's go," the mother said. "Let's not get involved."

"But why don't we help the good man, Mommy?"

"Don't stare like that – the police are only doing their job." She turned the child around. "Decent people don't get involved."

"What's decent, Mommy?"

"Look love, why don't we get you an ice-cream?"

"Yippee!" The girl dragged her mom by the arm. "One with chocolate and nuts!"

Rrekgetsi Chimeloane

They're coming!

MY MOTHER WAS SHAKING ME from my sleep that chilly August night. "They're coming! Did you hear that?"

"What?" I asked, hauling up my skinny twelve-year-old body from the floor next to her bed, trying to figure out what was going on. I was dressed in the old pyjamas she brought me from the white lady she used to do washing for, Mrs Drakeman.

Before I could make head or tail of what she was saying, she was knocking at the door of the bedroom next to ours. That was where my four older brothers slept. "Sello, Koliki," she called them in a whisper. "Tsotsi, Billy! You better wake up, there's something going on outside."

"What!" Sello asked in a grumbling tone from behind the door. The brothers knew that my mother was a light sleeper and heard almost everything that tiptoed around the yard at night. Her tendency to venture empty-handed into the dark Diepkloof night every time she heard strange noises around the yard, worried all of us a lot.

While I was still deciding whether I was dreaming or not, I heard a whistle blowing outside and a male voice shouting in the dark. "Mazulu ke a go!" He was referring to the hostel dwellers from Mzimphlope hostels. Mazulu ke a go, the Zulus are coming!

I shuddered. The stories I had heard from classmates made matters even worse. They did not talk about people being injured or sjambokked by the alleged Zulu impis coming from the hostels. They spoke about people being brutally murdered. I had heard that some people were beheaded. Some families were wiped out completely. When I heard the call in the dark, I felt an icy shiver running down my spine, just imagining all those things happening to my family. I had watched *Zulu Dawn* and had seen how Zulus fought against guns, armed only with their renowned traditional weapons, and knew that if we were faced with the same warriors, there was no chance of surviving the onslaught. And after seeing newspaper pictures of impis escorted by police hippos, my fear of the impis had become even worse.

"Where is Mma going now?"Tsotsi protested as he struggled to put on his pants in the dark, leaning against the frame of their bedroom door.

My mother unlocked the door and courageously stormed outside, empty-handed in her white night gown. It was such a dangerous thing to do! But since my father died a year before after a long illness, my mother had to assume the role of both parents, and maybe that is why she acted the way she did.

"Get her inside!"Thita, one of my two elder sisters who slept in the dining room, called out in frustration, almost shouting.

"Where is the candle?" Makhempe, the younger of my two elder sisters, asked.

"How can you light a candle under such circumstances?" whispered Sello. "Do you want the Zulus to see that there are people in the house, and kill us all?"

I was paralysed with fear. I had never imagined myself to experience such a situation at first hand. It was exciting to hear stories after the events had occurred, but it was a different matter altogether to be part of it!

My mother returned to the house. "Get dressed immediately," she ordered all seven of us. "People are running away out there. They are heading towards the mine dumps. We better start right now."

"What about Billy?" asked Koliki, one of my brothers.

"True. Billy won't make it to the mine dumps. We will go to Mma Motimele then," my mother changed her mind. "He'll be able to walk there easily. Billy, *ngwanake* – my child – get dressed!"

Billy had become physically disabled at the age of eight through a series of accidents. His left leg and arm were not functioning properly, so he couldn't walk as fast as was desired. Mma Motimele's house was only two blocks away from my home. She was my mother's niece, all the way from Phadi, next to Ramokokastad along the Rustenburg line. Her husband owned a Mini. They had only two children, a boy and a girl.

A brief, urgent meeting was held with the neighbours at the street corner where our four-roomed house stood. The decision was that all male children who were old and strong enough should remain behind and face the oncoming impis. They had to arm themselves with whatever weapons they had in their possession. It was a pitch-black night, and Diepkloof was not electrified then, being one of those locations termed "dark city". It was therefore imperative to have identifiers. So it was decided that during the battle in which they were about to engage, our men would wear white bands around their heads.

My brothers had already armed themselves with old golf sticks. I could not bear leaving them behind as the rest of us – myself, my two sisters, Billy and my mother – made our way towards Mma Motimele. I desperately wanted them to come along. I remembered the photograph in a recent newspaper, which showed a woman crying while her three boys were lying dead on the streets. I could just imagine those three boys being my brothers. What if they got killed? How could they survive against the fight machinery I had seen in *Zulu Dawn*? I would never forget some of the scenes across the plains of Isandlwana, in which assegais shining in the bright sun were piercing the British soldiers' breasts. There was no chance of my brothers and our neighbours surviving such an offensive.

As I looked towards the Soweto freeway, I saw red taillights following each other, bumper to bumper. Cars were getting out of Diepkloof. Our only hope was a Mini – and there were nine of us, together with Mma Motimele's family. That meant Mr Motimele would have to take two loads. The closest relative I knew was my grandmother, in Ga Rankuwa. In my young mind, I was planning that Mr Motimele – Papa 'o Nchimane as he was called – would be able to make two trips to Ga Rankuwa and back in the time it would take the Zulus to cover the 150 metres from my home to where we were, in Mma Motimela's street!

On the streets, people were streaming down towards the mine dumps opposite Zone Four, for shelter. Sleepy, bewildered children were crying as they were dragged along hurriedly through the dark night. I was so terrified I do not recall uttering a word, not even when we reached Mma Motimele's home.

Thantshi, Mma Motimele's daughter, and Thita, the eldest of my two sisters, were joking. "Look at what I have," Thantshi held out a long thick steel wire, "I will poke a man in his eyes if he comes next to me."

"You say eyes," Thita added. "Why don't you poke it in that large nostril hole like that of a horse?" The two of them laughed shrilly.

I looked at them and felt my knees tremble. What did they know about the Battle of Insandlwana? Did they realise that the warriors could just walk all over Zone Four, leaving anything in their trail dead? I shook my head, cowering in a dark corner of the house while the elders were contemplating contingency plans. I felt small and helpless, like a rat, nibbling at my fingernails.

30

My ears were searching, in the confusion outside, for the sound of the battle song. That was the sound that would signal the coming of our end, I thought. I did not know how to react in the face of impending death and destruction.

We waited and waited. There was a thumping sound in my ears – my own frightened heart. Around me the voices slowly subsided into a far-off drone …

The next morning I was woken by my mother's voice: "They're not coming any more. Come, let's go home."

I was so happy! I could hardly believe it … we were alive! The impis never came.

We watched people, mud all over their clothes, descending from the mine dumps, where they had sought refuge, abandoning their homes for the night. I laughed at them, forgetting how terrified I had been the night before.

We heard stories of boys who had put on girl's clothes, including panties, items they would normally hate to touch, for fear of turning into sissies. This was because they had heard that the impis had specific instruction to slaughter only male children.

Up to this day, I still have questions preying on my mind. Was there really a threat of the hostel dwellers attacking us? Or was it a prank by some deranged morons who wanted to see the whole of Diepkloof running up and down like ants? Be it as it may, at times I still wake from a half-sleep to hear my mother's urgent voice calling: "They're coming!" – and for a few seconds I become a panic-stricken twelve-year-old again.

Dianne Hofmeyr

Face of a killer

HE STARES STRAIGHT OUT of the photograph under bold headlines: FACE OF A KILLER.

Policemen swarm around him, holding back the crowd. People wave banners, straining to catch a glimpse of his face. Hands reach out eagerly. There's an aloofness about him that keeps him separate from the mob in the photograph. In the middle of the throng, he is still. The eye of the hurricane.

I am drawn into his vortex. My own vortex.

A smooth face. The clear skin of a twenty-year-old. Olive-toned. Dark hair cut close to the scull. It makes him seem spartan and strong. A gladiator. Yet at the same time, he seems exposed. Vulnerable. The bumps on his cranium show. He wears a nose-ring. I flinch at the thought of the needle piercing the fine gristle. Dark eyes reflect nothing. Searching his features, I look for some remorse. What do I expect to find in the face of a killer?

He stands upright. Square shoulders. Arms at his sides. Hands cuffed. Aloof. Emotionless. Isolated.

And those who glance cursorily at the photograph and headline, do they think of his mother, slowly tracing over the face of the boy she's given birth to?

My own mother ... what did she do?

The headlines then: WOULD-BE KILLER ESCAPES, over a smudgy photograph of a girl with straight black hair hanging to her shoulders. Black jeans with slightly flared bottoms. A tight black polo-neck sweater. A cigarette between the fingers of her left hand. A blurry, unposed shot, cropped by the editor to exclude the others. Someone's body sliced in half on the left of her. An amputated arm gripping around her waist on the right. The article stating: "involvement in unlawful activity", "in possession of restricted material" ... making it sound like polite porn!

Afterwards, when I was constantly moving, something drove me to phone my mother at regular intervals. There was that hollow sound to the phone. The strange clicking noise of a line being tapped.

"It's me ..." I'd say quickly, just so that she would know, before I put it down again. Other times I held the receiver tightly and stayed silent so that I could listen to her voice.

"Michelle, is that you ...?"

She'd wait to see if I'd hang up. Sometimes she started a tentative conversation.

"Don't worry, I'm fine. Aunty Gloria came to stay. I wish you'd come home. Are you eating properly?"

A small silence. Just the sound of my breath being recorded. What had she read into the eerie clicking of the empty space between us?

"What are you doing?"

Making bombs, Mom. Still making bombs.

"It's been raining today."

Did she sense my need to connect?

"There's a leak in the bathroom."

Then tentatively, "Michelle, are you still there? I feel a little silly ... I mean, talking like this ..." her voice trailing off.

A pause.

"Oh, damn these people."

Another pause. Expectant. As if she half-imagined the listeners might come onto the line.

Then an outburst. "Leave her alone can't you?" Shrillness and desperation in her tone. "She's my daughter!"

The months between phone calls stretched out. Eventually I gave up. There's not much point to one-way communication. I got tired of trying to find new phone booths in new places so they couldn't trace me. Never did she ask: *Why* are you doing this? What is driving you?

We became unconnected, my mother and I. And ever since Max, we stayed unconnected.

And when my photograph got into the paper, it didn't get any better. Why would it? I became free. My own person. Independent. My mother no longer had the ability to make me feel vulnerable. Neither could anybody else.

Or so I thought.

At school I was a passive child. My brother, Max, was the wild one. He was the one who climbed to the top of the loquat tree and broke his arm.

33

The one who stole sweets from the corner café, put a firecracker under Aunt Gloria's chair, stuck bubble gum into my cousin Lara's hair so that it had to be cut short. I was the one who picked up the bird that fell out of the nest in the loquat tree. Max was a year older but we were as close as twins born from a single-egg cell. He was my alter ego.

Then the envelope with its official stamp fell through the post flap. As it hit the passage floor, I sensed the bonds between us break.

Max read the conscription letter out loud.

I tried to fight it. "Say you're a conscientious objector. That you'd rather do service in a madhouse."

"But why? I don't have any objections. I want to fight for my country!" Then, with a smile … "And a uniform will suit me."

"It's not *your* country, Max. That's too greedy! And it's not even *your* war!"

And when he went on smiling … "They teach you to kill, Max!"

My mother was proud. She began to bake rusks. Bought tins of Hot Chocolate. Made up a sewing kit. Lots of khaki thread. Spare khaki buttons. Probably all the wrong size. A thimble as well.

"Max'll never use a thimble, Mom."

"It's just in case. He's not used to sewing and the needle will make a hole in his finger."

And his finger might just as well have been injured, for all that he never bothered to write home. I imagine he was too busy running up and down mountains with a full pack. But he sent photographs of himself in uniform. I passed them around my matric class. He was right. The uniform did suit him.

He came home after three months' basics, looking tanned and lean. Different. It made me nervous to be around him. Nervous that he was so at ease in his uniform, with the rifle slung so casually from his shoulder. But once he was sitting on the verandah wall in a pair of jeans and a beer in his hand, he was still the same old Max.

On the Monday when he left for the border, Max and I pricked our fingers and made a pact in blood, swearing all sorts of silly things. That when he came back, we'd travel. We'd conquer the world. Be famous. Invincible.

Halfway down the street, he turned and gave me a mock salute as I swung on the gate, "To honour and glory! To the defeat of the enemy!"

"Remember who the enemy is …!" I shouted after him. I don't think he heard.

34

The hole that was made in Max was much bigger than a needle-prick. The news came with a solemn knock and men with dour faces at the door. Max's name was unceremoniously tethered to a list of others on the TV screen, under a silhouette of a soldier holding a gun. His only glory.

My mother retreated into a tirade. The more she sobbed and recriminated, the tighter my chest felt. I didn't want her pain. I had my own. In the night when I heard her moaning through the thin wall between us, I pulled a pillow over my head.

I hated her for making me so vulnerable. *You encouraged him, Mom. You sent him off without any questions.* I had to blame someone.

I met Jakes at varsity.

It was a case of minorities getting together. Twenty or so years ago, a girl in a Chemical Engineering class of forty white males was as unusual as a black student. The classes were boring. I was looking for an escape. Jakes started inviting me to parties in Hillbrow.

It was impossible to know who the people were as we sat thigh to thigh in small, crowded, dark, smoky rooms. In the beginning I was silent and sullen. As the months passed, I realised the gatherings were meetings, rather than parties. At first I wasn't trusted. I was an outsider. Not party to the struggle. But slowly my seething anger filtered through to them. I was fuelled by determination to show the world I could take the place of Max.

Someone in the group had a manual that showed how different explosive devices worked. It seemed so straightforward.

Grenade: small explosive device. Fragmentation grenade: contains notched wire coil that shatters when the grenade explodes. Safety pin, safety pin ring, fuse, lever, filler, fragmentation coil. Nitroglycerin: principle explosive in dynamite. Detonating cap: set off with a fuse or electric current. Thermite: a mixture of aluminium and iron oxide used in incendiary bombs to start fires.

In our chemical pracs, Jakes and I nicked some stuff. I was happy for the first time in a long while. Making bombs was the most extreme thing I could think of to do. It was a vindication of Max's death. I don't think the reason really mattered to Jakes. As long as I was faithful to the cause.

A current of raw energy flowed between us. Energy that wasn't coming from working late and too many cups of black coffee. Sometimes our bodies touched, as we stood alongside the lab worktop. His arm against my arm, his hand on my shoulder, as he inspected something I was doing. It made me hold my breath and afterwards the space between us seemed spongy. One night as we were leaving and Jakes had his hand on the light switch, I saw the look in his eyes. Then we were plunged into darkness and my body melted under his touch.

Jakes and I made more bombs that year than the newspapers later credited us with. We didn't know all the details. Only what was meant to be blown up. A bridge. A power station. A supply depot. We were a formidable team. We could be trusted. We delivered.

One night they needed an expert detonator for a special job that had taken months of planning. The car had been parked outside the building for more than eight hours. The street was empty. We waited in the strange orange glow of the streetlights, our jaws clenched, hardened to the countdown. Jakes kissed me and I sensed his urgency.

Suddenly it was time. Then as if from nowhere, a truck swung into the street in front of us. I waved frantically to the driver to get out of the way.

The scene plays out in slow motion. The blast billows outwards. The truck and driver are shredded to pieces. A piece of shrapnel catches Jakes' temple.

The moment is etched into me. A second point in my life from which to measure time. Max and Jakes.

Looking into the face that I trace with my fingertips now, scares me. This blank, unreachable face.

I long to connect with this child gladiator. This boy of mine who has made himself invincible. I want to feel real flesh. I want to look into his eyes. Connect with him. I need answers. I want to know: Who is the enemy? Who's war are you fighting? Yours? Mine? Your uncle's? Or your father's?

Strange how easily my fingers remember the number combinations. The phone seems to ring interminably. Then I remember… my mother is twenty years older. It takes her longer to get to the phone.

I wait for her to pick up on the other side.

E.K.M. Dido

Baby

"NOOI!" MA'S SHRILL VOICE CAME FROM THE doorway of our two-roomed house. "Call your father, we have visitors!"

Wearily, I stopped playing, quickly throwing the ball through the hoop one more time. With Pa's help, my friend Toetsie and I had put the hoop up in the pepper tree so that we could play netball in the yard. "Who will Ma send on her endless errands if I'm not around anymore?" I mumbled under my breath.

I wondered why Ma was so excited. It was only Sergeant De Wit's yellow van that was parked at the gate. To me he wasn't a real visitor. After all, he also stays here in Nqamakwe, but in the area where all the white people live along with some of our people who are rich. He stays in that big green house with the red roof just on the other side of the stone church. Of all the people who stay that side of town he is the only one who occasionally comes to this side of town.

"Toetsie, quickly run home," Ma shouted at my friend. "Go and borrow one of your mother's good cups, I can't let my visitors drink from tin mugs. Be quick now!"

By now I was really curious about all this activity and ran down the footpath towards town where Pa worked at one of the general dealers.

When I got back home I couldn't wait to help Ma with the coffee. I was so eager to see the visitors that I stayed inside and helped pass around the coffee cups. The sergeant sat at the table, with a thin, bearded stranger. The man had his one arm around the shoulders of a girl who was probably a little older than me – maybe fifteen or sixteen. I kept looking at her. I had already seen many strangers from the city but never anyone like her. Her curly, black shoulder-length hair stood around her head hiding her small face. The blue eye shadow and red lipstick didn't suit her brown skin. Nor did her red fingernails. Her light yellow strapless dress was so short that it was pulled up high against

37

her thigh. It looked as if she was used to wearing a dress this length because she didn't bother to pull it down. But it was her light brown eyes that drew me to her face. They looked pleading and helpless, like those of the statue of the Virgin Mary at our church.

When Pa came home the sergeant introduced him to the two visitors, Attie and his daughter Baby. The sergeant said that he had been on patrol when he found the two of them next to their broken-down car.

"Doempie," said the sergeant and looked bashfully at my father, "since the child is almost the same age as Nooi I thought that I would bring them here so that she can a have a friend for a day or two. Just now, while her father was loading their luggage into the van, Baby told me that she really missed her mother. No one on the other side of town has any room for them. Neither do I. So if no one can accommodate them here then I will have to let them sleep in the police cells. But luckily your Ouma Stienie said that they could sleep in her front room."

Uncle Attie jumped to his feet, pulling Baby up with him. He held out his right hand towards Pa. "I'm a magician by profession. Maybe we can set up a show here before my daughter and I go to East London. That's where we live." He laughed loudly after each sentence and I listened as he told us how he and Baby had been on their way from Johannesburg to East London when their car broke down just outside our town and that it would be fixed by tomorrow only.

My parents agreed that they should eat at our house. Ma pretended to be angry when she said to the sergeant: "You don't have to look so bashful, Sergeant. It's an old tactic of yours to let people in need stay in any house that you fancy. Probably because you know that everybody here is prepared to do you a favour!"

The sergeant just smiled at her.

While the grown-ups were speaking I asked Baby whether she wanted to play netball. She looked keen but her father held her tighter and smiled at the sergeant: "Baby gets the fits and I am a little scared to let her out of my sight. Her mother and I have just recently decided that we have to get her to a specialist in East London when I get back. What does Daddy's girl say to that?" He hugged her shoulders tightly without looking at her.

I saw Ma frowning and I thought I saw tears rolling down Baby's cheeks. The sergeant left, promising Uncle Attie that he would tell everybody on his side of town about the magic show on Friday and Saturday. He would try to organise the hall for him.

Ma and Auntie Queenie went up to Ouma Stienie's house to make up the two single beds in the front room. I was dying to be friends with Baby. I wanted to brag afterwards that I had gotten a new friend – a girl from the city! But her father's arm stayed tightly around her shoulders. Later she asked her father whether she could go to the toilet. He looked at the curtain which separated the bedroom from the front room. Pa told him that the pit toilet was outside in the yard. As Baby got up, her father wearily lifted his hand from her shoulders and said: "When you come back, remember your pills, Sugar."

Only once Baby and I walked across the yard to the toilet did I notice how she swayed her hips with each step. This amused the children who had gathered at our yard. I went into the toilet with her as I always do with my friends. It was good that I did this because we had hardly closed the door when Baby started crying terribly and blew her nose on the hem of her short dress. Between sobs she said: "That sergeant didn't want to listen to me! I want to go home. I want to be with Mô!"

But when we came out again her tears had vanished and she threw her hips about again.

Later that evening I told Ma how Baby had cried but she just snorted and said: "Stay away from that ougat girl. That man's tongue is far too smooth and she hasn't been a child any more for a long time."

The next morning, Friday morning, we heard people shouting everywhere. Ma and I rushed out of the house. Ma was hardly outside when a woman screamed from the yard below us: "Tinkie, you heathen! What kind of sin do you let into your house by letting that naked child get dressed so that all the men in town can see her shame!"

Ma and I gave each other a puzzled look. I was wearing my faded everyday dress that comes just above my knees. Auntie Poppie from next door shouted at Ma: "Not your child, Tinkie. The child that came here yesterday. S'trues God, she is walking stark naked down from Ouma Stienie's house!"

When Ma saw Baby she gasped for air and held her chest. My eyes widened. I had never seen such a thing! Besides the pieces of pink cloth that Baby wore over her tits and around her hips she was completely naked. And it didn't even look as if her nakedness bothered her. She was smiling at everybody and waved her hands in a gesture of greeting as she stood there at our sink bath next to the house. All her make-up was washed off and now she looked very young. While Ma was still gasping for air, Auntie Poppie came closer to the fence to get a better view of Baby. "Lord, Tinkie, that is still a child!" she said. "And she looks like someone who has had too much to drink!"

Even though she was smiling broadly, Baby looked strange. Her eyes were torn wide open and she looked as if she wasn't seeing anything in front of her. But she didn't smell of wine. Ma and I pulled her into the house and Ma told me to quickly get a blanket to cover her up. But this was a problem – every time we got the blanket over her head she shouted: "Mô, help me!"

When Baby's dad stormed breathlessly into the house Ma began scolding him: "Look, I don't want to tell you how to raise your own child but this girl is so pissed that she can't even say Ma correctly. And it's still early in the morning!"

He tried to get hold of Baby but she hid under the blanket and clung to Ma for dear life, screaming: "Mô! I want Mô!"

Baby's dad was getting angry with her. She didn't want to come out from behind Ma and he said he would beat her till she was dead. Then he took a small plastic bag from his pocket. It contained some pale, flecked pills. He held it up for Baby to see. She looked at the packet and made a feeble attempt at grabbing it from behind Ma's back.

Her father shook his head as he sat down at the table. "Oh, Missus. I don't know what I should do with this child. Now you can see why her mother doesn't want to be near her when she is like this. She went and stole the pills for her fits and drank too many. Sugar, come to Daddy."

Ma pulled Baby from behind her back and pressed her into her father's arms. Then she began crying just as pitifully as Baby had done. I was probably the only one who noticed that as soon as she was back in Uncle Attie's arms Baby stopped crying. Instead there was a look of terror in her eyes.

That whole day Baby's thin body stayed right next to her father. Even when she had to go to the toilet, it was her father who stood outside and waited for her. All the women were talking because Ma told them what had happened that morning at our house. "Man, that man's wife is lucky! Our husbands can learn something from him about how to love their children."

But that afternoon when the sergeant and his wife came to our house everybody forgot about Baby. In all the years they'd been living in Nqamakwe, Sergeant De Wit's wife had never set foot in the coloured area and now she arrived with a plate of cake for Ma's visitors.

Ma was so shocked that she didn't know what to do. "Nooi!" she shouted as she came out the house. "Go and borrow a cup of sugar from next door so that I can give Missus Sergeant something to drink!"

I was sitting under the pepper tree scouring pots and wondered whether Ma had gone completely mad now and so I shouted back: "The sugar is in the box under my bed, Ma!"

I was dying to know what they were talking about but I realised I had better stay outside. All I could hear was Sergeant De Wit promising to organise the hall as he was leaving.

The sergeant and his wife had hardly gone when Uncle Attie walked hastily to town with Baby to see how far his car was. They were back soon. Baby was smiling broadly but Uncle Attie grumbled impatiently that his car was not ready yet. Why does it take so long! The more he grumbled the more Baby smiled – such wide smiles. Later she laughed and chatted with us, at first shyly and later loudly. But every now and again she quickly glanced over at her father. When Ma asked what her mother's name was Uncle Attie stopped complaining about his car and pulled Baby closer to him. She kept her mouth shut and Ma frowned.

Late in the afternoon when Pa came home he had a message for Uncle Attie from the sergeant. Uncle Attie should just wait there and the sergeant would bring the keys to the hall himself later.

Uncle Attie was so happy that he jumped up, pulling Baby with him and then he did a few dance steps. "Baby, we are on a roll!" He laughed. But Baby's eyes were wild. She looked scared.

Later when the sergeant came to our house, his wife had joined him again. I was amazed because this time she had brought a packet of sweets. I stayed close by. Uncle Attie jumped up and stretched out his hand to greet the sergeant even before he was inside the house. "Thanks for the break, sarge. I need every cent to pay for the car. And this baby of mine can really sing!"

Sergeant De Wit stretched out his hand towards Uncle Attie, and before the other man could even blink he had handcuffs on his wrist. He started shaking and suddenly he was crying loudly.

But the sergeant spoke even louder. "Attie Barnard, alias Andrew Barnard, I hereby am arresting you for the abduction of Claudine Grootboom and for providing drugs to a minor."

Ma and Pa also spoke loudly: "Sergeant! What are you doing now?" asked Pa. "Who is Claudine?"

"Sergeant, couldn't you put the handcuffs on outside the house? You'll bring bad luck for ever!" That was Ma.

41

But the Sergeant wasn't listening to my parents. He was busy with the handcuffs. His wife sat holding Baby tightly, rocking her to and fro. Baby was sobbing and holding onto the fat upper arms of the sergeant's wife. She clung even tighter when Uncle Attie glared at her and stepped towards her. But the sergeant pushed Uncle Attie out of the door. I went and stood in the doorway and watched them. The sergeant was holding Uncle Attie by his elbow and was pushing him up the hill to where the van was standing. Uncle Attie was trying to resist, kicking the dry, pale sand, sending the dust flying. But the sergeant was hefty and strong and he pushed Uncle Attie into the back of the van.

When Sergeant De Wit was finished with Uncle Attie he came back to us and gave my parents and Baby, who was still clinging to the sergeant's wife, a calm smile.

"Doempie and Tinkie," he said, "my wife is the one who worked it out. You see, see is from Pretoria herself. She was very curious about this child who says "Mô" instead of "Ma" and so she came along with me yesterday. It was she who put me on the right track. Only people who come from the Transvaal say 'Mô'. This is the missing child from Pretoria," he said, pointing at Baby. "For the last two years, her face has been on every wall and lamppost. The poster has been up in our office too."

Jenny Hobbs

Dog star

I REMEMBER THE EXACT MOMENT when I first wished to turn into a dog. It was in the middle of the afternoon and I was hanging over our front gate, trying to get as far away as I could from Ouma's muttering, when I saw Loretta coming down the road. She was stepping around the potholes which were still full of muddy rainwater when this brak whined at her from the alley by the bottle store.

You know the kind of dog I'm talking about: all scraggy grey fur, starving and slinking and unwanted. Except by Loretta, who was crazy about dogs. All dogs. Any dogs. She had three of her own and was a sucker for other people's. Dogs were attracted to her too; I'm sure they have an instinct for people with SPCA engraved on their hearts.

Like this brak that day. It whined at her and she squatted down right there in the road, never mind the mud all over her skirt, and started to pat it and lay on the sweet talk until it had its mangy head in her lap, looking up at her with googly eyes.

That's when I first wished I could be a dog, so I could get sweet-talked and put my head in Loretta's lap. She's beautiful but looks down her nose at me, even though we used to be best friends when we were kids. After our folks got moved to the sub-economic housing, our two next-door semis were far out on the Flats where the Port Jackson willows started. There were hardly any other kids around. Me and Loretta were buddies, riding our broomstick horses and building sandcastles that she decorated with fynbos flowers – too lovely.

But then it became time for school and the girls didn't play with the boys. After that it was only, "Howzit, Fanie?" if we passed by each other, and when I got glasses and my nose and ears and legs wouldn't stop growing, even that stopped. Loretta wouldn't so much as even look at me. But if I was a dog, I thought, she'd let me put my head in her lap – maybe even kiss my nose and scratch behind my ears with her long red fingernails.

Ma says I'm too dreamy, it makes people idle and useless, but I couldn't handle life at home if I didn't escape into my head sometimes. She's got to be the stroppiest mother on the Flats, old Eagle Eyes. She put in fifteen years of hard labour as a till operator at Pick 'n Pay before they promoted her to supervisor, and now she queens it over the rest of the staff, all of them poep scared of her.

So a skinny dweet of a husband and two small kids had no chance. Pa started to drink: Klipdrif at first, sliding down to bakleiwyn and white pipes on the dirty stoep behind the bottle store after he lost his job. One day he walked in front of a train and got so mangled she could only identify him by his bloody overall. For months after his funeral, the kids at school screeched, "Toot toot! Peanut butter!" every time they saw me or my sister Petal. It made her cry, but I couldn't. I just learnt to switch off and dream.

Ma fought the tendency tooth and claw. She decided early on that Petal and I were both going to be teachers because it was a respectable profession with a good pension at the end. So we were klapped without mercy through school: homework done before supper or no TV, swotting for tests, extra lessons if our marks fell under a B. Petal got a place at training college the very year they started retrenching teachers because there were too many. When Ma read about it in the papers, she was whipped out of college into a bank, and now she's a teller.

That left me cowering under Ma's gale force ambition for me to rise above the semi-detached, the gang fights outside the bottle store and the squatter shacks packing ever closer at the end of our road. All the Port Jackson willows are gone; now it's a human junkyard built of corrugated iron and old signs and plastic that bangs and flaps when the wind blows.

Ma wants me to be either a lawyer or an accountant. "Take your pick, Stefanus," she reckons, "I'm not fussy. Just don't be too long about it. I want us to move to Sea Point when you qualify for a housing loan. I can retire there happy."

"And what about Ouma?"

"With any luck she'll be dead and gone by then."

"Shame, how can you talk like that?"

"Easy," says Ma. "You don't have to get up in the night to change her wet sheets."

She could talk. I had to mince up all Ouma's food and wheel her to the pension payout queue and listen to her non-stop muttering when nobody else was at home.

Which was why I was leaning over the gate that day, wishing to turn into a dog so's I could make out with Loretta. What kind of dog should it be? I wondered.

A Doberman? Too aggro. A bulldog? Too fat and wrinkly. A border collie? Too nervous. A foxy? Loretta already had one, called Sporty. A Maltese? Ditto, called Snowball. (Loretta wasn't good at original names; the third one was a cross-eyed Peke by the name of Cutey Pie.) A Great Dane that looked like me, long-faced with gangly legs that go all over the place every time he thumps down? She'd hate it on sight.

Then it hit me: I'd be a ridgeback. Noble and powerful like a lion with a well-muscled body, yet good-tempered and (most importantly) African. Loretta was so patriotic she never went anywhere without her New South Africa flag done in beads and pinned on somewhere. She'd be blown away by a ridgeback.

There must have been a genie lurking in a bottle nearby (there were a lot lying around because of the bottle store), because that very night I found myself whining and scratching at Loretta's front door, begging to be let in.

The brat pack sensed competition straight away. Sporty was at the other side of the crack under the door in a flash, sniffing, "Who are you?" then growling, "Go away!"

Snowball yapped, "Push off, fleabag. You're not wanted here."

"Why not?" I whined. "I'm cold and hungry."

"This is our porzie," Snowball snarled. "Home, sweet exclusive home. Get lost."

I heard the Peke toyi-toyi up on manicured paws. "What's going on here?"

"Just a passing brak." Sporty gave a contemptuous snort.

"Lazy good-for-nothing. Vamoose, stink-arse!" Snowball yelped.

I hadn't realised what a foul mouth he had – not surprising, I suppose, with only a few rotten teeth left. Loretta should have called him Halitosis.

Cutie Pie was dancing up and down yipping, "And don't darken our door again, you horrible thing."

Sporty barked, "That goes for me too. Hit the road, Jack."

I had expected some opposition but not wholesale rejection. So OK, I know I'm no oil painting in real life, but people who know me (Ma and Petal, anyway) say I've got a great personality. Match it up with a ridgeback's looks and I should be a winner. Encouraged by the thought, I notched up the decibels so Loretta would hear me over *Egoli*.

That how I got her away, by moaning and howling like the Southeaster through the cracks in the walls. I heard her say, "Sounds like somebody's in trouble," and the door opened and the brat pack came screeching out, jumping up and yapping round me, strings of saliva flying like fishing lines in the snoek season.

They tried hard, those hounds of hell, I'll give them that. But they were no match for my suave good looks and world-weary eyes. "It's a ridgeback," Loretta sighed, dropping to her knees and gathering my head against her blouse where I nuzzled in ecstasy between billowing breasts. She was really stacked. This was more like it.

"Get your snout out of there!" Snowball launched a vicious rearguard attack but I just lowered my haunches, trapped his squirming head and went on nuzzling.

"Aren't you a beautiful boy, then," Loretta crooned. "Where do you come from, Diddums?"

I raised my head enough to murmur into the lacy recesses of her bra, "The name's Hond, Fanie Hond," but she didn't understand. Loretta's forte was body language, not Dog. No matter. I could put up with Diddums, so long as I got regular meals and petting and a top dog's privileges, which would hopefully include a place on or very near her bed.

Well, it worked. The brat pack were totally eclipsed by the love affair that blossomed between me and Loretta. She'd never had a big dog as a pet before and she thought I was Mr Canine Right: a noble warrior from Central Africa bred for lion hunting, all hers to command. She made a show of checking to see if anyone had lost me, but of course nobody had.

Being doted on by Loretta was great. She bought me a big round basket with a soft cushion and my own aluminium dog bowl. She taught me tricks and when I remembered them, gave me choc-chip biscuits and called me "good boy". Best of all, she let me put my head in her lap whenever I pawed her knee and I could leave it there as long as I liked.

The brat pack were wild with rage because they'd got used to taking turns on Loretta's lap. They surrounded me as I lay on the front step one morning when she was out at work and her Mom had gone to town.

"You're a pervert!" Snowball seethed.

"Disgusting," Sporty snorted. "Dogs like you should be locked up for the good of society."

46

"In chains! And whipped!" Cutey Pie darted forward to give me a nip and I brushed her off, sending her rolling into the cactus bed.

"Don't do that to my friend, you son of a bitch!" Snowball stood up on his hind legs trying to threaten me, every bone in his body vibrating with fury. 'Vuilgoed! Farting flea factory!'

"Swine. Bully." Sporty wasn't as verbally gifted as Snowball, though he was a good jumper. He had vaulted onto my back and was worrying my ear with needle teeth, trying to draw blood.

I swatted them both away to join the yelping Cutey Pie and put my noble head down on my paws for a snooze. It would take them a while to bite out the cactus spines. This was the life. I'd never had it so good.

The only thing Loretta wouldn't let me do was shove my nose into her crotch, by way of friendly greeting. "Nice doggies don't do that," she said, pushing me away the first time I tried. The next time she tapped me on the nose and when I tried it again, she actually smacked it. "I said *no*, Diddums. Bad boy."

The brat pack were rolling round on the carpet yapping with glee so I showed my disdain by stalking off into the next room and ignoring Loretta until she came to beg my forgiveness. She had a soft heart as well as amazing breasts and unbelievable thighs. I felt like Hugh Hefner during the lamplit nights in her room when she undressed and admired her body in the long mirror, front and back and sideways, shadow and curve, soft padded cushions on the hips and – this was a surprise – a butterfly tattooed on one shapely buttock.

I'd lie in my basket pretending to be asleep but watching my private strip show from under my eyelids. The best part was the creaming ritual: she'd rub her face and neck with night cream, her hands with hand cream, her heels with heel balm, then – the high point – her generous breasts with firming cream, round and round until I was panting. Then the gossamer nightie would go on and she'd slip into bed and drop a sweet-smelling hand to fondle my head as she drifted off to sleep.

I was in paradise, man. I wished it could go on for ever, but of course it didn't. Loretta began to say that I was such a gentleman (howls of mirth from the brat pack) that I must be pedigreed, and got books out of the library to check my features for good breeding. One day she said to her Mom, "Maybe we should take Diddums to the dog show? I'm sure he could win prizes."

"Good idea. We'll feed him up a bit more and enter him in the Con-course d'Elegance."

Loretta's Mom was very refined. She was always carrying on about how vulgar and pushy my Ma was, which made me growl when I heard it. It takes a lot of guts for a widow to bring up two kids and make sure they get educated, and to look after her dead husband's gaga old mother, all on her own. She didn't sit around crocheting bead doilies all day, she hakked the till operators and shelf packers and counter staff in her supermarket to the point where her managers boasted about their keen workers and productivity figures.

The brat pack took the idea of the dog show very badly, specially as their baskets had been demoted to the kitchen. Cutey Pie began to hyperventilate and have panic attacks. Sporty got morose. Snowball's last few teeth broke off in a sneak attack and he had to eat bread and milk and tinned kitty fish. When I started calling him Puss-Puss he went ballistic. Malteses may look fluffy and innocent but they've got a mean streak to them like all terriers; they'll always go for your knackers.

The Saturday of the dog show came. For weeks, I'd been fed like a king and exercised by Loretta, who devoted most of her free time to grooming and training me in the back yard. As I trotted down the road by her side in the sunlight, I was looking magnificent, even though I say it myself: smooth and sleek, with rippling muscles set off by a new leather collar with a chain lead. As we passed the gate of my old home, I saw Ma pushing Ouma up the path looking dead tired and thanked my lucky stars it wasn't me, though I felt guilty too. Shame, they had no man of the house now.

I turned my noble head away so I wouldn't have to feel bad on such a special day. It didn't smell so good, though. The municipal workers were on strike again and the rubbish hadn't been taken away for three weeks so the braks from the squatter camp had torn open half the bags and dragged their contents all over the show, hence the terrible pong. I picked up my paws like a quarter horse as I stepped round the rotting piles, afraid of being contaminated or cutting one of my pads on broken glass or an open tin.

"Careful now, Diddums," Loretta was saying, "you don't want to get your beautiful coat soiled. Watch out for that ash. Mind your tail on the barb-wire. Don't let the chain drag in the dust."

There was a howl of mockery from the front stoep of the bottle store. Too late, I remembered the K9 Gang that sometimes hung around there, scratching their fleas and hassling passing bitches and fawning on their leader, a vicious Rottweiler cross by the name of Ratface.

"Hey, Diddums!" he snarled. "You a moffie then, all decked out like that?"

I strained at the lead to try and make Loretta go faster, but she wanted to keep me calm and clean for the show. "Not so fast!" she said, holding me back. "We've got plenty of time. Watch out for those rusty nails. If you go near any vrot meat, I'll be very cross."

"How can you let a woman push you around like that?" Ratface snarled. "Are you a dog or a mouse?"

"Moffie. Moffie." The other gang members had prowled to the edge of the stoep. "Let's see you vastrap, fancy-balls."

I turned my head and barked, "Voetsek!" hoping it would stop them jumping down long enough for me to get Loretta past and away. I was bigger and stronger than any of them, but if they all attacked at once I'd be in for the high jump.

"Voetsek?" Ratface was stalking down the steps, bristling. "Are you telling me and my chinas to voetsek? That's just asking for trouble." He crouched in front of me, head and throat covered in scars, mean eyes, lips drawn back over long yellow teeth, baying like the Mouille Point foghorn. "I'm going to donner you up, Diddy-boy. Rip out your guts for garters."

I planted my paws on the ground, heart hammering, and felt the lead's cold chain slither down my neck. Only then did Loretta wake up to the situation, and I must say she surprised me. In one quick movement she pulled a small canister out of her pocket and sprayed Ratface with tear-gas. He cringed away, whimpering and pawing at his eyes. By the time she turned towards the rest of the K9 Gang they had fled up the road yowling, mangy tails between their legs.

"You shouldn't try and mess with a girl from the Flats!" she shouted after them, then knelt to comfort me. Some of the teargas had caught me too and I was wheezing and gasping, my face on fire and my eyes streaming.

"Never mind, Diddums," she soothed, patting my shoulder. "We'll forget the dog show. Sit up and ..."

"Sit up and drink this, Fanie." Ma was tapping my shoulder, bending over me with a medicine spoon. "You've got a fever but the doctor says it's only the flu. Sit up now, there's a good boy."

I turned my noble head on the pillow that was damp with sweat, and howled.

But I'm glad to say that the dream didn't go to waste. The very day I'm better enough to get up and hang over the gate again, Loretta comes walking up the road and I call out, "Howzit, Lor."

"Don't even ask," she says, nose in the air and not stopping.

So I tune her, "When did you get the butterfly tattoo done?"

"What?" She stops and swings round with her mouth open. Catching flies, Ouma used to call it when she still had her marbles. "How do you know about my tattoo? Not even Mom knows."

"I've got my sources." Thank you, Mr Sandman.

"Have you been looking through my window at night? Shame on you, Fanie." Loretta might be beautiful but she's getting to sound just like Ma.

"Nooit," I scheme, "you should know your ou pel better than that."

"How else would you know?"

"Ever heard of a ridgeback called Diddums?"

That gets her guessing. "How much?"

I give her my smoothest smile. "Never mind. But listen, how could I see in your window the way you keep your curtains closed so tight? Ask yourself that, poppie."

Revenge is sweet, hey. Every time she passes by now, she checks me out with suspicious eyes that really look at me. Me, Stefanus, man of the house, future lawyer or accountant, I haven't decided which yet. I'll never make it into the movies, that's for sure, but Ma and Petal reckon my great personality will take me far.

Fatima Dike

Only the number has changed

AFTER ALL THESE MANY YEARS, a few words exchanged with an old man at the taxi-rank this morning have caused me to think differently of my mother. I think I understand her better now.

I had a mother who was amazing in ways that my young mind never appreciated. Though she was not well educated – she had to leave school in standard five – my mother was the one who taught me how to survive in our country.

As a young girl she used to work on a Mr Brown's farm. Her job was to clean the farmhouse. But though she was the one who cleaned the floors, Mrs Brown never allowed her to enter the farmhouse kitchen wearing her shoes. So she would leave her shoes outside.

When my mother married my father, they went to live in Langa, which in those days was run by the Cape Town City Council. On the main road, next to the police station, some white families lived in a couple of cottages. The men from these houses worked for the City Council. They were responsible for the day-to-day running of the township. Directly under their command there were wardsmen, called *izibonda*. My father was one of those. The izibonda were go-betweens for the people of the community and the white people who ran the township. In the evenings at 7 o'clock, they used to go around the township on bicycles to switch on the street lights. In a sense, the wardsmen were also social workers in our community.

My parents arrived in Langa just as the township was being built, and my mother considered herself fortunate to be employed soon afterwards as a maid by Mr Rogers, the superintendent of Langa. My mother brought up Vera and Maureen, the daughters of Mr and Mrs Rogers. She worked for the family for thirty years, until the beginning of 1961, when the Group Areas Act was implemented and all the white people had to leave the township. Mr Rogers decided to retire, and he went to live in St James.

The connection between my mother and Mr Rogers in the years after his retirement was Thomas, who had been Mr Rogers's gardener. If Mr Rogers wanted to convey a message to my mother, he would phone the City Council in Langa, where Thomas found a job after the family's departure to St James, and leave a message with Thomas. Then Thomas would get on his bicycle and come to our house. He used to knock on the door, and wait for my mother to call him in. He would then take off his hat and make a point of cleaning his shoes on the mat. Exactly as he used to do at Mr Rogers's house when he was still gardener there – a job my mother got him.

Every year, precisely one week before Christmas, Mr Rogers would call Thomas. Soon after Thomas arrived on his bicycle. He would put his bicycle against our fence, wipe his feet, come inside and say, "Annie, the Master has phoned. He said that I must tell you that he's going to come and see you the day before Christmas."

At the time my sister and her husband were running three businesses in the township – a supermarket, a butchery and a service station. I was a qualified butcher, working in the family business. After that message my mother would call me at the butchery and tell me to prepare a leg of lamb. It had to be the best meat, because the Master was coming. I used to get so sick. I used to get SO SICK! I could not understand what tied my mother to that man, especially now that she no longer worked for him.

I would take this leg of lamb to our home on the appointed day, and my mother would make me wrap it in brown paper and write on it in a black copy pen: *Mr Rogers*. She wanted to be sure that nobody in the house would make the mistake of cooking this leg of lamb. She would then wrap it in plastic and keep it in the fridge until Mr Rogers arrived.

On the morning of Mr Rogers's visit you would sense by the atmosphere in the house that somebody very important was coming. My mother would take out her white apron, starch it and put it on. She would pick out one of her best tablecloths and put it on the table. All the special things that Mr Rogers loved would be on the table. And when the Master arrived he would park his car on the pavement right against the fence of our house. And my mother would not wait. You should have seen that woman flying down the stairs to meet her master. When he stepped out of the car, he used to go to the boot, and inside the boot he would have a huge tray of plants, because my mother loved plants, and she always had a beautiful garden. She would quickly rush over and take the tray of plants from the Master, because she would never allow him to carry anything.

And the two of them – there was such happiness between the two of them! They would walk into the house and then sit down to have tea, with my mother serving him. And they would chat! What was it about the two of them? How could there seem to be such harmony in a relationship that I perceived as so uneven? Was my mother still bound by the fact that this man used to be her master for thirty years? She still called him Master Rogers! That I could not swallow.

So this ritual took place for many years. Year after year the Master would come, the leg of lamb in the fridge, the tray of plants, the tea ...

But the anger in my heart never died. I could not understand why my mother was treating this man as a friend after thirty years of working for him as a maid. Sometimes, in those early years in Langa, she even had to go to his house to look after Vera and Maureen while he and his wife went out for the evening.

Then civil war broke out in Zimbabwe. My mother wouldn't miss a single news reading on TV, because Vera and Maureen were by then married to farmers in Zimbabwe. After the news, my mother would walk outside, mumbling, "I wonder what's happening to poor Vera and Maureen." I would get SO angry, I would say to my mother, "Wake up! It's 1977. Black youths are being killed on the streets by whites, and you worry about two white girls who would never have the decency of writing even a postcard to thank you for carrying them on your back!"

My mother just turned around – you could see the lioness in her eyes – and she would say, "SHUT UP! There are things you will never understand." And I would shut up.

"Why do you still call him Master when you don't work for him any more?" I asked my mother one day. My mother turned around and said "SHUT UP!"

And I shut up.

I kept being shut up every time when I tried to understand what was going on. Here was a white man who had paid my mother very little, to whom my mother had given her working life, and thirty years later she still adored that man. As a child and as a young girl I could never reconcile myself to that.

And then one day, long before Christmas, Thomas came on the bicycle. He put the bicycle against the fence, knocked and cleaned his shoes on the mat. And then Thomas told my mother that the Master had passed away, and that the Madam, who had never phoned before, had phoned that day to tell him to tell Annie that Mr Rogers had passed away. I must concede, I was happy. But the two of them were talking in such soft voices, you could *feel* the hurt.

My mother wanted to know when the Master was going to be buried, and Thomas told her. "Are you going?" my mother asked Thomas. When he said that he didn't have transport, she said, "Just come here and we'll go together."

After Thomas had left she changed completely and started bossing us around. "Phone your sister!"

I did as she told me, and when the phone started ringing, I passed it to her. "Nomahlubi," my mother told my sister, "the Master has passed away and he's being buried Wednesday next week at ten o'clock. I want you to bring your car around at nine."

End of story.

And so, the following week, there was my mother, dressed to kill, and Thomas, being taken by my sister (in a champagne outfit as a send-off) in her 380 Mercedes Benz to bury the Master.

The year before my mother died we were driving around Langa one day, because my sister, when my mother couldn't walk any more, used to drive her around to see all the old places. Driving down Church Street, my mother said to me, "Do you see that house, Fatima? When your father and I first moved into this township, we got work with Mr Rogers and he gave me this house. It was just a two-roomed house, but he told me that when my family grew bigger I could come to him and he would give me a bigger house."

I couldn't help saying to her, "Wake up, these are government houses, he could give you any house he wanted."

And Nomahlubi, my sister, said, "Shut up, idiot! Black people stand in queues for fifty to sixty years trying to get houses. And Mr Rogers made this easier for your mother."

I shut up.

A few months later my mother asked Nomahlubi to drive us down Bennie Street. "Do you see this house?" she asked. I said, "Yes." She said, "When your brother Benjamin was born, the house got cramped with

54

three children, and Mr Rogers moved us from the house in Church Street to this one."

I shut up.

Of 796 Mendi Street, where her youngest child was born and where my mother spent the rest of her life, she used to say, "So kind of Mr Rogers to move us in here."

What could I say?

The old man to whom I spoke at the taxi-rank this morning happened to have known my father and my mother. "Yes, your father was a wards-man in those early Langa days," he said. "Ah, that Mr Dike, he was a man. And your mother ... I knew her well. Your father used to get ac-commodation for us new ones, but looking for jobs was difficult. Then he would send us to your mother. We would go round the back at Mr Rogers's house and she would give us bread and tea in the kitchen. Be-cause she was close to the white man and she was such a good worker, she was able, through him, to get work for your father and for many of us at the municipality, you see?"

Yes, I do see after all ...

My fingers lovingly trace the brass number 18 on the front wall of the house where I have lived for fifty-two years. The house where I was born, and where I still live with my children.

Only the number has changed.

Daniel Bugan

A Sunday out

REGGIE AWOKE FROM THE COUCH in the front room. It took a few moments for him to realise where he was. The flat was quiet and filled with late Sunday afternoon shadows. He dragged himself onto his feet and stumbled off to the old people's bedroom.

The old man lay under the bedcovers. His wife sat on a chair next to him. They did not touch or say anything to each other. They stirred and brightened when they saw Reggie in the doorway.

"Hey, Reggie, you're up!" the old man said happily. "Sit down, won't you? Woman, get Reggie a drink."

Reggie sat down groggily in the chair facing the open window. The old woman poured him half a glass of Virginia from the rotund caraffe on the dresser. She filled the rest of the glass with ginger beer.

"This'll help for the heavy head," she said, handing him his drink.

"Where's Mitchell?" Reggie asked.

"He's still asleep," the old woman said. "We can't get him up. Mavis phoned here a couple of times already. I told her I haven't seen him today. You know how she can get."

"The nagging bitch!" the old man said. "I don't know how he can stay married to that woman."

"So where were you two the whole day?" the old woman asked. "You must have had a good time, the way you look!"

He recalled the blurred stops at the shebeen; the driving around nowhere for some time, drinking with friends; and the ever-present scavenging, corrupting women. All the things not worth repeating. So he said, "Oh, around. I don't remember much."

"You must be hungry?" the old woman asked. "Can I warm you some chicken?"

"Don't ask, woman," the old man said. "It's not polite to ask."

"I know, but maybe he doesn't feel like eating."

"Chicken'll be fine, thanks," Reggie intervened.

The old woman left and went into the kitchen.

"I'm really glad you're awake, Reggie," the old man said. "Now at least I have someone intelligent to talk to. I can't talk to anyone here."

Reggie smiled cautiously. His mind felt incapable of any constructive thought. All he wanted now was to go home. He was not in the mood for Mitchell's father.

The old man, lying there with his pot-belly straining the covers, beamed expectantly. The Sunday papers lay strewn across the bed and on the floor. On top of the cupboard old newspapers, read and analysed during the idle hours of the week, were stacked in an unruly pile. Reggie was aware of the old man's passion for political debates, of how he lived for moments to test his wits against that of his guests. His arguments were radical and controversial – daring to be defied and ready to defy.

"I read in today's paper about that Steenkamp character alleging that Boesak was in on that scam," he started enthusiastically. "Do you think Boesak's capable of it?"

"A guilty man would say anything to save himself," Reggie countered safely.

"Still, I think he's in for it this time. His mistake was divorcing his wife for that white woman. White people's lifestyles are more expensive than ours. The poor man probably couldn't keep up."

The old woman walked in on their conversation. She held out a side-plate to Reggie, piled with roast chicken, potatoes and vegetables.

"Is he at it again with his politics?" she asked. "That's all he's good for these days. Got his nose in those newspapers all the time. Only gets out of bed to go to the toilet."

"I'm an old man," the old man said. There's nothing outside *there* for me anymore. All I need is my newspapers and books. My children have brought me nothing but trouble and disappointment. I'm just waiting for God to come get me. And I hope He hurries!"

"Don't talk like that," the old woman said. "Not in front of other people, anyway."

"Oh, shut up, woman! What do you know about these things? Reggie understands. He's a learned man. Why don't you just pour us another drink?"

They sat in reflective silence as the woman busied herself with the drinks. It was very dark outside by now. From where he was sitting, Reggie could see the lights of the tiny apartments crammed into the mud-coloured building opposite. Multi-coloured curtains, some decorative, others crude, distinguished one household from another.

"You better eat up," the old woman said to him suddenly. "You probably haven't eaten anything today yet, you poor thing. You young people don't eat when you drink. Mitchell's the same."

He started eating obediently.

"Where's the drinks, woman?" said the old man. "How do you expect Reggie to get his food down?"

The old woman handed them their glasses. The old man took his and slugged it down, pulling a face. He took a wedge of orange from a saucer standing on a little table next to his bed. He chewed and ate the fruit hurriedly, and spat out the taste into an enamel pot at the side of the bed.

"Diabetes," he explained to Reggie. "The fruit kills the sweetness of the wine."

Just then their youngest daughter came in through the kitchen door. She looked unkempt and she seemed upset. She hesitated slightly when she saw Reggie sitting in the door of her parents' room and then smiled timidly, almost apologetically, for her slovenly appearance. She ignored her father and motioned to her mother to follow her into the living room. Her mother got up with an apprehensive sigh and followed her inside.

"What the hell is it now?" the old man called after them. "I don't want no trouble in this house! Woman, don't let that bitch bring her trouble into this house!"

The two women ignored him.

"I don't know why the Lord punishes me like this," the old man said.

The old woman came back into the room. She looked as if she had been crying. Her shrivelled mouth pursed tightly in her set face.

"That rubbish don't want to give the child back to her," she said. "He had the child for the whole weekend. Now he says the child don't want to come back."

"Fine! Let the boy stay with him," said the old man. "He wants to be with that bastard anyway."

"I wish Mitchell was awake," the old woman said. "He'll know how to sort this out. Do you remember how Mitchell beat that rubbish down the stairs the last time, Charles? He's really scared of Mitchell."

"Where's the girl now?" asked the old man.

"She went up to go reason with the rubbish again."

"I don't want her causing a scene here," the old man said. "That's all I'm telling you, woman." Then, turning to Reggie: "That girl has been nothing but trouble to us and she's not even twenty yet."

"It's ever since that rubbish got her pregnant," the old woman explained. "She was only sixteen when she had his child. I don't know what came over her. He's not even much to look at and he's got children all over the place."

"Scum!" the old man said. "That's what he is. No-good scum!"

"No man would want her now," the old woman continued. "She's got nothing to offer. She's spoilt goods. She'll only get all the rubbishes now."

"It's this place, you know," the old man said. "It kills everything. It's killing me."

"Don't you want her?" the old woman asked Reggie. "She likes you. I can tell she likes you."

"Don't even think about it, woman," the old man said. "You can see he's a man of education. A teacher. What'll he be doing with something like that?"

"I'm not a teacher," Reggie said.

"You're not? He looks like a teacher, doesn't he, woman?"

She nodded. They were not interested in knowing his real occupation. They were happy with their illusion.

The Sunday night was getting on now. The noises outside subsided respectfully. Reggie wanted to get home to the safety of sanity. He wanted to escape the chaos and hopelessness which surrounded and choked him here. It scared him that some of the people here seemed to be so comfortable with it. He wished Mitchell would wake up and take him home. But in the meantime, sitting there, the reality of tonight and tomorrow tugging at his mind, he consoled himself with the drinks offered by the old man.

He competed half-wittedly and half-heartedly in the old man's political debates, feeling his strength and enthusiasm fade. The young girl came in by the kitchen door again. Her blouse was torn and her upper lip split and bloodied. This time she was too upset to be timid and walked right into her parents' room. She did not look at Reggie.

"He hit me!" she said to her mother. "He says I'm a whore! He says Robin doesn't belong with a whore like me."

"The bastard!" the mother said. "Who does he think he is?"

"It's because you drink with any no good bastard who buys you a beer," the father said. "Who knows what that leads to?"

"He still can't call my child a whore!" the old woman said. "I didn't raise whores!"

"Just wait until Mitchell gets up," the girl said. "He'll make him sorry. I told him Mitchell's here. He's really scared of Mitchell."

"Maybe we should call the police," the old woman said. "We can get him for assault."

"It's no use," the old man said. "The police won't come. They never do. You have to be dead first. Let Mitchell fix him up."

Reggie was quiet. He looked again at the lights of the flats across the road. Flats just as small and cramped as this one and, very likely, with households equally disturbed and depraved. In the soft light of the street-lamp he could just make out the name of the block nearest to him. Its nameplate, "Stuckeris Hof/Court", hung lopsidedly on the side view of the building. Reggie stared numbly at it for some time.

Then suddenly, from the back room, came the thick, rugged sounds of someone waking from a deep sleep.

"There!" the old woman said excitedly. "Mitchell's up at last."

"Now we'll see who's a whore," the girl said, looking expectantly at the door.

They were all quiet as they heard Mitchell come stumbling in from the back room.

He looked at them with blank, bleary eyes and uttered something that got stuck in his throat. Then his body jack-knifed and crashed onto the nearest chair – a disconsolate heap of creased, sour-smelling clothes.

"I'll walk home," Reggie said and got up.

MOSES SOVUMANI MAHLANGU

Mr Cellular

DURING MY TIME ON THE MAMELODI campus of Vista University, you'd have been a laughing stock if you did not know about Mr Cellular. Seriously speaking, you'd have been thought to belong either to Vista Soweto or Vista Sebokeng. Only a handful on campus, the most ignorant ones, were unaware of the presence of this campus Adonis. Who was he, this Mr Cellular? Ingoapele Tlhoaele, Bachelor of Arts student and a Psychology tutor, was nicknamed Mr Cellular because he was the first on the Mamelodi campus to be clutching that irritating technological device: an eminent figure whose popularity went beyond the boundaries of the Psychology department, which was the largest community during our years.

He was one of the *Romanos* on campus, those guys with the many girlfriends. In fact, the most outstanding Romano. Believe me, it was no child's play to be a Romano. But whenever *mamgos* – gossipers of the campus – were listing campus Romanos, Mr Cellular would come out tops.

Few students knew Mr Cellular's real name. Some of them knew it from attending first-year classes with him, just before he acquired that tormenting technological device. Also amongst those who knew his real name were his fellow homeboys and girls, the folks from his hometown, Ga Rankuwa – a township known for the enormous Medical University of South Africa, commonly known to its folks as "Garakas". But to the rest of those on campus, Ingoapele was known as Mr Cellular.

To me it wasn't clear what really made Mr Cellular such an outstanding Romano. I'm not sure whether it was his physical appearance, his fluency in English, his charming personality or his brilliant brain.

Mr Cellular was beautiful. What? We Africans are not supposed to say males are beautiful, are we? As the Zulu wedding song says: *Ubuhle bendoda ziinkomo zayo*, a man's beauty lies in the heads of cattle he pays for lobola. But I don't care what one should or should not say. Mr Cellular was beautiful. He was dark in complexion and had a spotless face, a captivating smile and smooth kiss-hungry lips. His physique would have made you swear he was a frequent visitor to the gym. But no, not Mr Cellular. This was his natural body.

While some of his former high school mates from Mmanotshi-Moduane, in Heilbron, were struggling to express themselves in English, Mr Cellular's English flowed like the Toloane River. You'd have sworn by your long dead father that he was the product of a private school. His accent outwitted that of Tshenolo, of the famous *Gaabo Motho* TV series. And he was well aware of his own command of the language.

I remember asking him how and where he had acquired such a good command of English. "Mlotjwa, it's easy. Reading, reading and more reading makes one good at a language," he replied with confidence. "When I'm talking about reading, I'm referring to heavy stuff. The work of Ngugi wa Thiong'o, Chinua Achebe, Thomas Hardy, D.H. Lawrence, William Shakespeare, William Wordsworth ... South African works by masters like Gomolemo Mokae, Kaizer Nyatsumba, Es'kia Mphahlele and Ellen Kuzwayo. And reading doesn't stop there – there are the daily newpapers, the Sunday newspapers, the magazines ..."

With regard to acquiring an American accent he said one should frequent a cinema and acquaint yourself with television. Although I bought his idea about the sources of good English, I was not impressed by his second idea. I, Mlotjwa Ngoma, an Ndebele boy, wasn't interested in picking up an American accent from television soapies and talk shows. No, not me.

Mr Cellular was always elegantly dressed. He was "expensive" – township jargon for those whose clothes carried desirable labels such as Carvelle, Jonathan D, Etienne Aigner, Bass and Bruno Magli. He wore *ubucwebe* – chains, rings and bracelets – all over his body. From the scent of the perfumes he used, you could tell that he must have dug deep down into his pocket for them.

Academically, Mr Cellular was a giant. He passed his two major courses, Psychology and Sociology, with distinction. Whenever Mr Cellular was present, any lecturer who had come to class ill prepared, bragging to the students, as often happened in the Psychology department, would leave the lecture hall tail between the legs.

Although the majority of students were impressed by Mr Cellular's academic prowess, a handful of individuals were not. Not surprising, as one man's meat is another man's poison. The unimpressed were Law and Commerce students. Those were the students who claimed to be doing better, more difficult and prestigious courses on campus. They used to say Mr Cellular excelled because he was doing easy courses. This amused me because the same Mr Cellular outwitted them at most of the campus students' mass meetings.

As a student who was also registered in the looked-down-upon Faculty of Arts, I understood Mr Cellular's fate. Like him, I was not bothered by those who used to say I was doing "female courses", because I knew what I wanted in life. Like my friend Mr Cellular, I often outsmarted them in our chatty debates, regardless of the subject on the table. We in the Arts read much more widely.

You'd wonder how I, a typical Ndebele guy from KwaMusi village in the KwaMhlanga region of Mpumalanga province, came to befriend Mr Cellular. A "cheap" chap from the dusty streets of KwaMusi befriending such an "expensive" lad from the famous Garakas? Yet, to us it was simple. As Sociology students we were brought together by the dictum, "no man is an island – interaction carries you through". We were both doing Psychology and I was a tutor in Sociology. Our offices were next to each other in the Social Sciences Building.

I give credit to those scientists who invented contraceptives. If it was not for the existence of a loop, a pill and the most reliable of them all, the French letter, Mr Cellular would have completed his BA degree simultaneously with BB – Bachelor of Babymaking. During vital student occasions on campus, such as the Freshers' Ball, Pre-Exam Bash, Stress-relief Bash and the Spring Bash, one would really see that Mr Cellular was a big bug when it came to the ladies. Once they had acquired Dutch courage, those ladies known as "occasional drinkers" would exclaim in unison, *"Beshe ke hyona, Bjwala buteng. Bana batlile. Mr Cellular keBoss!"* "It's bash time. Booze is available. Ladies have come, and Mr Cellular's tops!"

Among Mr Cellular's girlfriends there was only one lady whom I happened to know by name. That was Tintswalo. She was a first-year Psychology student and hailed from Bushbuckridge. Tintswalo was the prettiest in Mr Cellular's "choir" – as I called the group of ladies surrounding him. She was neither tall nor short, just in between. Her peach-red complexion made one doubt her Shangaan origin. She had a sharp nose, ever-shining eyes, milky teeth and perfect legs. Wait! Her smile was of its own kind, incomparable and inexplicable. It just killed softly. Most importantly, she was the only lady with an ever-clean-shaven head on campus. Surprisingly and disappointingly, Mr Cellular claimed not to love her because she was just a beauty without much grey matter. In fact, he used to say, "I pursued Tintswalo only out of greed. Although I have an insatiable appetite when it comes to ladies, I hate ever-smiling ladies who are good listeners but show no innovation."

Mr Cellular had a surplus amount of self-confidence. He knew he could pick and choose.

Then one Thursday, just a month after we had come back from our winter vacation, I saw Mr Cellular packing all his belongings from his office. Playfully, I asked, "Hey my man, where to? Have you been promised a better office in the lecturers' block?"

"Things are bad, Mlotjwa. I'm kissing this office goodbye. The Psychology department has …"

"Suspended you? Sacked you? What?" I asked before he could finish.

In a shaky voice he told me the department had fired him. When I asked for more details, he said, "Please help me clear the office first."

I helped him eagerly, hastening the clearing process so that I could be fed with the full details of this incredible story. It was unbelievable that such misfortune could befall a man like Mr C.

"Mlotjwa …" Mr Cellular began hesitantly while we were sitting in my office.

"I'm listening, my friend," I encouraged him to continue.

He told me that he was sacked because of a scandal unveiled by the department. "I suppose you know that I love ladies, and more importantly, beautiful ones. Although it is easy to hook them, it has not been easy to keep them," he sighed, adding, "I have done the most risky things just to keep a lady in the register of my beauties, unbelievable things. It is difficult to tell you what happened, but I'll try – sooner or later, the whole campus will know anyway."

I kept quiet, not wanting to disturb him. Responding to my attentive listening, he said: "I don't know about the Sociology tutors, but the Psychology tutors have access to test question papers for the classes we are tutoring prior to each and every test. We are the ones who take original question papers to be photocopied, take the copies back to the department and count them, in preparation for the next test."

I started to see direction in his story. Did he really take advantage of the situation and sell the question papers?

He denied having sold any question paper. "I only gave those who asked for them. For the past six months things were running smoothly until Monday, when Tintswalo approached me. Although I know that she is struggling with the course, she has never asked for a question paper before. It was the first time. Without any suspicion or hesitation I gave her a question paper for the test that was supposed to be written today. On Tuesday, the unexpected happened. She came back to blackmail me. She told me that she was aware of the whole campus's knowledge that I don't love her, but am just using her. She told me she was not the fool I thought her to be and she was going to teach me a lesson I'll never forget. She demanded one thousand rand in cash or else she would let all hell break loose.

"In desperation, I made some threats myself, but she just laughed, saying she didn't care what action I wanted to take. She had already photocopied the question paper and had given copies to her four friends who would be witnesses if anything happened to her."

Mr Cellular paused for a moment. "The day on which I was supposed to give her the money was yesterday, at noon. I failed to meet the final deadline of half past three. Firstly, I was not convinced that she would have the guts to execute her threats. Secondly, I was not prepared to pass on such a huge amount of money to a parasite.

"Today, at about quarter past nine, ten minutes before the scheduled time for the test, I was called urgently by the Head of the Department. When I arrived in her office I nearly died of fright. There Tintswalo was, in the office of the Head of the Department, with her friend Tsakani. It was clear that they had come to spill the beans – copies of the question paper were spread out on the table. I was summoned to a disciplinary committee, comprising of the Dean of the Faculty, and all other members of my department. The committee accused me of exchanging question papers for sexual favours and took a joint decision that I should resign and vacate the office within an hour."

When he finished, I was already soaking with sweat. "I've learnt the hard way," he ended his unbelievable story.

Mr Cellular stood up and left the office. For good.

The beautiful Tintswalo was certainly no fool.

JAMES MATTHEWS

Little savages

FROM THE MOMENT THE CAR PULLED out from Shortmarket Street,
Shane sat silently at the window, taking in streets not yet filled with the
usual Saturday morning rush. As the car swept onto northward-bound
Voortrekker Road, familiar scenes and buildings passed behind them.
Then they slipped out of the city, and miles of road seemingly without
end stretched ahead of them. Shane was fascinated by the open spaces,
so unrestricted by parallel and criss-cross streets. The enclosed wheat
fields bordering the road were cleared of their crops, given over to grazing sheep that hopped stiff-legged at the sound of the car engine. A
horse outlined on a slope, its mane stirred by the wind, caused Shane to
hold his breath. A hawk was silhouetted as it glided on a current of air.
The recurring peaked hills, catching Shane's gaze, were so different
from the grandeur of Devil's Peak. He glanced at his uncle seated next
to him and gave silent thanks for being the favoured one, selected above
his brothers and sisters to join his uncle on this trip to the countryside.
Already, he felt far removed from the tenement houses overflowing with
people.

The car slowed down as they passed through the main street of Cale-
don and then into the farmland area.

"This is Teslaarsdal," Shane heard his uncle say. The car peaked a
steep slope. Down below were clusters of cottages nestling in a valley
enclosed by hills. The car eased into the straggly sand track bordered
by white, lime-plastered cottages. On both sides Shane could see pro-
truding roofs of similar cottages flanking the track. His uncle stopped the
car in front of one of the cottages. Shane followed him to the doorway. A
man seated next to the doorway rose at their approach, hand raised in
greeting, a smile on his face. Inside, it was cool. The floor had the gleam
of darkly-shaded linoleum, but it was made from something else, not the
wooden strips like at home either. Shane felt as if he had dropped into a

pool of water after too long in the burning sun. He looked up shyly when he was presented, then sank down to sit stiffly on the edge of a chair, eyes flickering to the framed photographs on the unevenly plastered wall.

He stole sidelong glances at the man and the woman of the house. The man was wearing a white shirt without a collar, and the turn-ups of his corduroy trousers hanging above his farm boots were a good six inches wider than Cape Town fashion demanded. The woman wore an ankle-length black dress, shiny with age. Her hair was hidden under a floral doek.

The flesh in their faces was pared away, the skin stretched tightly across their cheekbones. They seemed to look past their visitors as if at some distant object. Behind them, he caught a glimpse of two boys, about his own size, who hurriedly withdrew their heads when they became aware of his scrutiny.

After he had finished his coffee served in a thick, white enamel mug, his uncle told him he should join the two boys who had left while the visitors were served by their mother.

Shane's eyes took in the surroundings. Everything filled him with delight: the broad sand strip leading from the crest of the hill down to the valley and which seemed to serve as a main street; the white plastered cottages with their thatch roofs placed without any semblance of order; the gardens in front of the cottages offering an assortment of vegetables which he had previously only seen piled on a hawker's cart, the loquat and quince trees spaced in between; the stream of cold, clear water skirting the gardens; and patches of greenery everywhere giving relief to the eye. Even the sky was different. In town, with its narrow streets and crowded houses, it seemed as if the sky pressed down on everything. Here the sky had an immeasurable spaciousness.

The two boys he had seen inside the house were joined by three more. They stood at a short distance from him, looking him up and down, seemingly taking note of every item of his clothes: his white crew-neck shirt, his new blue jeans, his baseball boots, and perched on his head at a jaunty angle, his linen cap with its exaggerated peak. The other boys wore khaki shirts and trousers – their feet were bare. Shane looked at them scuffling the sand with their heels, an itch developing between his own toes.

"Can I play with you?" Shane asked tentatively. No one answered. He took their silence for acceptance. He joined them when they walked away.

Suddenly, they glanced at each other, then whirled and raced up and down the open space in front of the houses, like colts released from their paddock, heels kicking at the sand and letting out neigh-like shrieks. They would come to a halt briefly, then turn about wildly and take off on their mad gallop once again, finally collapsing in a heap.

"I could've run some more if I'd wanted too," the biggest boy said.

"Me too!" "And me!" two voices hastily added.

Then they stared at Shane, as if they saw him for the first time. "What is your name?" It was more of a challenge than a request.

"Shane."

"What kind of a name is that?"

The five boys sniggered as if they shared a secret which excluded him. Shane was puzzled by their reaction to his name. His mother had named him after the hero in a western film. They changed position, heads drawn closely together, voices soft, but not soft enough for him not to overhear. "Where did he get that funny hat?" he heard someone whisper. How could he tell them that in Cape Town the offending cap was *the* thing to wear? Then he had another idea. He moved next to them.

"Do you go to the movies?" he asked no one in particular. They looked at each other for confirmation and the one who had made clear his superiority as a runner, nodded his head.

"I saw a movie three months ago, when we went to the dorp. It was in the kerksaal," he said.

"Why the kerksaal? Isn't there a movie house in the ... dorp?"

"No, but there's a movie every Saturday afternoon in the kerksaal."

"Where I stay, the bioscope is open every day. It's just some streets away. I go every weekend," he informed them. "And sometimes during the week if I find enough empties to sell." He took note of their puzzled look. "In Cape Town, you can sell empty wine bottles. You get money for empties."

They sat enthralled as he told them of the pictures he had seen. Most of the names he reeled off were unfamiliar to them.

Only Willa, the leader, seemed unimpressed. He probably was unhappy about the easy manner in which Shane had turned their hostility into friendship. "Come on," he ordered the others, "let's go hunting paddas at the vlei."

He turned towards Shane and grudgingly said: "You can come with us, if you want to."

Shane nodded happily. This was something to tell back home. Padda hunting was something he had never done before. For that matter, he had never seen a frog apart from pictures in a book.

Two mongrel dogs joined them as they set out across a field.

He spotted it the same time they did. A small, sleek two-toned pig came waddling towards them on its short legs. Shane burst out laughing. He had never seen a funnier sight. It reminded him of a drunken sailor on his way to his ship after drinking in the shebeen in Berg Lane.

Willa took hold of the dogs by their necks and shoved them in the direction of the advancing piglet. "Vreet hom, Tiger! Get him, Rex!" This made the other boys laugh. Then Willa released the dogs and they charged at the piglet.

Tiger bowled the piglet over. The two animals were a tangle of legs. The piglet was screeching in an agonizingly high pitch. The other dog snapped at the piglet's flank as it jumped up to trot away at a pace Shane would not have thought possible, screeching all the time. The boys, with loud shouts, blocked it off and turned it back towards the dogs. The cries coming from the piglet quivered through the air, above the screams of the boys and the sharp barks from the dogs.

Shane stood transfixed with horror as one of the dogs got hold of the piglet by its ear and sent it ploughing in the soft sand. The piglet screeched like a one-stringed violin plucked at by a demented fiddler.

Shane grabbed a stick from the ground and rushed at the dogs, hitting at them. With startled yelps of pain, the dogs ran out of reach of his stick. For a moment, no one spoke. Shane watched how the piglet, in its fear, ran full-tilt into a paling fence and bounced back. Then it was out of sight; only its screeching could be heard, tearing through the afternoon air.

The stick was violently jerked from his hand, taking some skin off his palm. "Why did you hit my dog? Why did you hit Tiger?" Willa, eyes fierce, demanded angrily.

"They were biting the pig."

"It is our pig!"

He looked at them. Their faces held the same cruel expression as when the dogs were mauling the piglet. He could almost feel their teeth sinking into him.

He felt a blow on the side of his head before he could explain. It came from Willa. Shane raised his hands to protect himself as the others joined in. They dragged him to the ground. Pain struck at several parts of his body. They left him on the ground and ran off, jeering. A trickle of blood dripped from one nostril and his cap was on the ground, its peak torn off.

Tears flooded Shane's eyes as he cursed them. But it made no difference. They were savages anyway.

Luke Alfred

Dad's funeral

(An extract)

WHEN GAVIN EASED THE VAUXHALL IN under the big elm it must have been about seven or so. I remember that it was beginning to get dark. As we were taking the luggage out of the boot I noticed Grandad sitting silently at the top of the steps, his face hooded in darkness. Mom and Gavin didn't notice him until they were almost face to face with him and their chatter, tumbling lightly in the summer air, immediately came to a stop.

"I think you'd better sit down," Grandad said tenderly as they approached, so softly that the words were hardly spoken. I felt sorry for Mom later because although I knew something was wrong she still hadn't realised that anything was amiss. She half-turned to Gavin and I could see that she thought that it was almost funny, as though she had just won the crossword or some secret relative had left her money in their will. Part of her was still caught in the journey and the car and the summery weekend away with Gavin and me. Her face still wore that questioning expression when she read Boet's telegram under the back light; the telegram telling her that Dad had overturned the Ranger on the road to Kokstad and was dead.

Grandad provided us with details through the evening as we all got drunk slowly on a flagon of Tassies Mom kept in the fridge. But for then – for that moment – I could only watch as Mom's body fell away from her and crumpled, just as an exposed section of cliff would collapse and crash into the ocean. As for myself I wasn't sure what to feel but I know that swimming around in there somewhere, in the tumult and the eddies of numbness, was excitement, as though something very special and worthwhile had just happened to me, something that made me stand out and separated me from the boys in my class.

Later I felt a pain that clawed itself out of me but somehow couldn't bring itself to leave. So it clung to me all evening, pulling at me and making me bleed. I had no idea that Dad could die so suddenly, could take himself away like he did. It seemed a peculiar way for him to go, without explanation or goodbyes. I thought of his five rand, the five rand with which I had tried to buy beers in the lounge bar of the train, but was turned away because the bartender told me I was under-aged.

Mom sobbed until she was exhausted and then, when we all thought she had cried out her love and pain, she would cry some more. It was a long night, difficult for Gavin; a challenge for Grandad, who never stopped being considerate and kind, boiling the kettle, bringing Mom a shawl, filling the glasses; and a strange one for me. I knew that it was the most important night of my life but I couldn't seem to digest the fact that Dad was dead. And so we huddled through the gnashing, the silence, the heavy words that rolled like boulders from the mouth. No-one could bring themselves to state the obvious, not even Grandad, who to me was the bravest of us all.

We all knew that Dad was drunk when he rolled the car. This thought hovered around us like a curse all night – as we sunk deeper and deeper into the kitchen chairs, sinking onto our elbows until our heads lolled forwards on our necks.

There was a small collection of strangers standing at the graveside, some trying to shake the awkwardness from their shoulders, others trying to make their hands smaller than they seemed. We noticed a priest and a pregnant woman (who we guessed was Betty Duvenhage) and a man we suspected was Eddie Botha, Dad's boss at Koo. As we approached, the man stepped out to meet us. "Eddie Botha at your service, Mrs Scott," he said, his delivery sharp and quick, and it occurred to me that he was the type of man who was in the habit of selling people things they didn't need. "If there's anything I can do, really, anything."

Mom knew of Eddie because they had spoken on the phone before we left Cape Town. Eddie had sent the driver to meet us at the Durban airport and it was Eddie who had Dad's final possessions, his wallet, his last packet of Luckies, his matches, his salesman's file. Mom had gossiped about Eddie during the flight. Before one of their conversations, she said, as the Koo switchboard was struggling to connect her, she had overheard a voice saying he'd rather be fishing for kob than going to the funeral of a soutie who spent too much time in Kokstad and Port St Johns. Eddie's voice, Mum suspected. She tried to make light of it but I knew that it bothered her. Mom knew that when Dad got into a bar he was the most popular guy in the world, but once he left it he was his normal lost self, a man that had one foot in reality and the other in a place that neither of us could name.

Following on Eddie's heels was a priest who introduced himself as Father Sweeney. His expression told me he was trying to be brave about a situation he didn't care for, but he chatted to Mom, a film of fake interest filling his eyes, fishing for words to describe a man whose troubled grace he would never know. After a time he called us together, his voice not quite under control. We bowed our heads in prayer. Out of the corner of my eye I looked around and saw a bedraggled group, unconnected by even the remotest of threads. It reminded me of Dad's first AA meeting that night at Umhlanga, the coming together of strangers. A night when the world had seemed blessed with hope and I, a mere boy, was aching to know what was about to happen. And now we were here, listening to Father Sweeney tell half-truths about a man who was neither my Dad nor anyone else I had known, and Dad was dead, his body heavy in the cheap coffin that Mom had borrowed money from Gavin to pay for.

As Father Sweeney tried to get a purchase on my Dad, I wondered vaguely about Dad's failure to get a purchase on life in South Africa. It was a country in which he lived and died but never quite seemed to believe in, except perhaps when we were playing cricket against England or Australia. For a moment I wished that he could have hammered together some kind of makeshift peace with the blacks and the Afrikaners. Not because he liked them but because he realised that fate had thrown them together and the smartest thing to do was to accept them for what they were. Like him, they were blundering onwards in search of better things, and he surely knew that whatever their differences, they shared blood and bile and, like him, their smiles told the story of how good it was to be alive in the world.

I wished, most of all, that Dad had lived his life in such a way that a few more people gathered to honour his passing. In a place beyond words I envisaged the people of Durban lifting cold black receivers to their ears and dialling friends' and colleagues' numbers. "I don't know if you remember Brad Scott? Well, the poor bastard rolled his car just outside of Kokstad," they would say before gathering breath. "He was dead when they found him. I saw in the paper that his funeral is tomorrow afternoon at two. I'll be going – just to pay the respects." Here the voice would pause, unable to ask if Des would want to come along, and punt into recollection instead. The recollections would depict Dad as a fine, bold man – carefree, happy, filled with conscience when conscience was called for. Several such conversations would be played out across Durban and Umhlanga, hot news skidding through the wires; there might even be calls to Stanger and Umzinto, kerbside conversations, calls to the newspaper where busy men would catch themselves and change direction – finding a sentence or two of soft civility somewhere within. People would talk about him on the practice green at the bowls club and in the tea-rooms and the needlepoint classes. And although he wouldn't be famous, he would be remembered with fondness and pride. My Dad.

On the day of his funeral people would take their best shoes from the bottom of their cupboard and give them a quick buffing up; they would shave more carefully than usual and spend a quietly reluctant half-hour over the ironing-board. Then, the gentle echo of the iron still spitting in their thoughts, they'd have a quick sandwich and cup of tea and get respectfully into their cars. Feeling the unspoken weight of the moment they would gather at the graveside, surrounding the piles of tangy earth, looking at the sky and trees with new eyes. As Sweeney's words washed over them they would set sail for the sea of memory, remembering Dad's column in the paper, his kind words, the time he remembered the birthday of someone they had assumed he had forgotten – the time that he managed to smuggle their son's rugby result into the smalls, past the attention of the editor.

But that wasn't my Dad. My Dad attracted two sub-editors from the paper, men who Mom guessed had come along on the off chance that they'd be able to filch some free eats afterwards. There were nine of us in all and although I don't remember thinking about it that day, I'm sure I assumed that the surroundings were as they had always been. They were not filled with poetry or poignancy and were nothing other than themselves. Nine mourners was the best that Dad could do and it made me feel so wretched, so blighted with pain, that had I been able to pass into nothingness by holding my breath then I would have held my breath for as long as it took.

We spent the next few days sorting through Dad's possessions, selling off the furniture and drinking lots of tea. We were less careful than we'd been when we visited the flat before the funeral service but we were still aware that Dad's spirit was hovering above us, so the first couple of hours we whispered, just in case we were overheard. We put things into boxes, wrapped everything in newspaper (even when we didn't need to) and wiped every surface at least three times. Sometimes we became lost in a memory, thick and rich, remembering events we hadn't thought about for years.

While we were clearing the bathroom, putting everything into the Omo-scented boxes I was given by the owner of a nearby cafe, I noticed a jar of Bay Rum hair gel. I unscrewed the lid and smelled the jelly. It lifted me back to a city barber shop that Dad had taken me to on our weekend in Johannesburg. Capri Gents Hairdressers, I think it was called. The barbers were grumpy, chain-smoking Italians who seldom talked but nodded their heads instead. Occasionally they rolled a sentence or two of what we suspected was English in their customers' general direction. As we stood in the doorway Dad put his arm around my shoulders and bent down. "The secret with these guys is not to be offended," he said, his breath heavy with nicotine. "They're gruff, but they mean well. Smile at them if you don't understand what they're saying and leave it all to me."

Dad told them that my hair was getting wild. He wasn't having me looking like some young hippie, he said while winking, and it was time to take it all off. He smiled and asked for a light and we both knew then that they wouldn't turn us away for not being one of their regulars. I rather liked him being bossy. I remember being surprised because I would have expected him to have found a chair and told them to get on with it before opening his paper as wide as it could go; he would then dive straight in, sinking into the words and pictures like the father I knew. But he didn't sit down. He stood there and watched the barber at work. At first, when the barber used an electric razor, he didn't seem to mind Dad standing nearby. But then he moved onto scissors and comb and I could feel a tremor in his hands. I knew exactly why the tremor had happened, but I was glued to the chair, looking straight ahead. I couldn't tell Dad anything. I stared at the vials of pink liquid and the brilliantine, the pairs of scissors and combs in a row, the glass chest of cut-throat razors; I felt the shop's cool poise, the marble surfaces, the busy blur of the fan as it juddered through the air overhead, the electric razors dangling from their hooks. I sat and waited. Eventually the barber ordered him to sit down. "Sit down, down," I think he said, "it's not so good you stand."

Afterwards we stayed at the back of the shop, watching, my haircut making me feel attractive and easy to love. Dad was sitting next to me, his elbows resting on his knees, his mind pulling him forward. Both barbers were dressed in white jackets and both of them were smoking, their cigarettes relaxing in a nearby ashtray. As we watched, Dad spoke softly, pointing out things I could see but had not yet learnt to describe.

"What is their secret?" he asked.

I shook my head and half-smiled. I remember being intrigued but I had no idea of how to answer. I fidgeted in embarrassment. For some reason I wanted to giggle. I could feel bits of hair underneath my collar and across the top of my shoulders.

"Their secret is that they neither bend down nor reach up. They make sure their customers' heads come to them. When they need to adjust the chair, they raise it. When they get a shorty like you, they put you on a board across the chair's arms."

I nodded and smiled because I knew he was right.

"They have another secret?"

I smiled again. The scene was suddenly intimate. I had goosebumps all over.

"Well?"

"I can't think, Dad."

"That's okay," he said, and squeezed my knee. I looked at our reflections in the mirror, sitting in our wood-panelled alcove, the magazines dense and still in their nearby pile, the ashtray with its upturned cup at the end of a long silver leg. "Their problem is that they must work all day. Because they're on their feet for so long each day, they have to ration their energy. They have to be careful how much they do. Their secret is the care that they show. Carelessness is a way of spilling energy, so they are careful, quiet, unhurried. They have to work just so." He paused to let it all sink in and then he turned to me and raised his eyebrows as if to say: "And that's not all."

"Actually they have many secrets," he continued. "Their care works in three ways: they care for the customer, they care for themselves and they care for each other. Barbers must always show care. If they nick a customer here, it's a disaster. Everything is thrown off balance. They'll have to swab the cut, apologise. Maybe he'll be angry; they'll have to placate him. There might be words; he might never come back. So they are careful: careful towards the customer, themselves and each other. Care is what keeps their world together."

I never knew that Dad could think like this. I laughed because I understood instinctively that what he had said was true. Without putting it into words I understood that he had reached my heart – he had blessed me. When I stood up my legs didn't feel strong. I had to breathe deeply. Part of me wanted to cry; another part of me wanted to scream with joy. I remember being giddy with love.

Elsa Joubert

The key

AUTUMN MAKES EVERYTHING look even more drab. The unswept leaves in the driveway, the yellowing poplars rustling drily in front of the double garage.

"Just listen," he said, as if it was still strange to him that so many birds nested in the trees in front of the house in which he had grown up. "My mother always said that it drove her crazy." The birds chirped ceaselessly, like giant cicadas, the same endless noisy chirping.

The whole day he had been delaying coming here for the last time. He constantly found other important things he wanted to do, and now it was already late in the afternoon. He opened the car door so that the young woman could get out.

"Come," he said and strode up the stairs of the verandah. At first she hesitated, looking at his shadow jumping up the stairs with him, breaking at each step.

Beyond the chattering of the birds one could hear the sound of the traffic from the nearby highway. With the key that was still on his key ring he unlocked the fancy front door – all cast iron, glass, wood and chrome. "Come," he said again. "Let's go inside. They have probably left already."

But from the back of the house, at the end of the passage, they could hear the sharp sound of a young woman's heels on the parquet floor, occasionally muffled by a carpet underfoot.

And then his mother was standing in the entrance hall. "Why did you only come now? We have been waiting for you since half past four. Now it's too late, we have to go." She wore shiny earrings on her small lobes, her hair well groomed and her perfume dark and sweet.

He could hear his father's footsteps. "Good day, son." And then he greeted the young woman. His father was standing behind his mother, his hands busy with his collar, pushing the top button straight. Something he always did when they were going out on weekends and he didn't want to fight with his wife.

"Come inside," his father said, stepping back.

The young man said nothing. He just walked down the passage, passing the woman who held out her hand to touch him – come and rest under my hand, the hand that is so used to touching your body, her eyes pleaded. But he evaded her touch.

"I've come to bring my keys and I want to fetch my scuba gear from the cellar."

"You said you would come at four." The shrill voice of the woman was resentful. "And now you come when we are just about to leave." She looked at the young woman who was with her son. Just like she had looked at her many times before. "Are you doing this on purpose?" she asked wordlessly. "Do you come here with your dirty sandals, your unkempt hair, your face not made up, just so that I can see that after all that he is used to with me, he prefers you?" Unconsciously her eyes moved down the passage towards the elegant sitting room, "He comes from a home like this and now he moves in with you."

"We don't want to keep you," the young woman says, shifting her chewing gum to the other side of her cheeks. "We'll just pull the door shut behind us when we leave." She shrugs: "Or do you want us to go out through the back?"

"I'm coming to pick up the last stuff." He was wearing a slightly dirty, bleached jersey. He looked thin and young in that jersey. Is he still so young that his sleeves are too short for him? his mother wondered. Is he still growing? She couldn't bear the thought. Her gold bangles were pushed back against her wrists and she pressed her fingers together – the nails filed and painted, pecking like the beak of a bird at her husband's pulse: "Come, we're going to be late. You know they are waiting for us."

She quickly adjusted her well-groomed hair in front of the mirror in the passage and licked her lips. Her nails cut into his wrist. His hand covered her fingers protectively, maybe warningly. His eyes rested on his son. He had taught him to scuba dive.

"If the light in the cellar doesn't work, you know there are spare bulbs in my study."

"It's all right, Dad."

When his mother and father had gone out the front door he took the key from his key ring and put it on the desk in the study. The key ring felt lighter without the keys of the house. He threw it into the air and caught it with his palms wide open and then he put his arm around the young woman. "Now for the scuba gear. I'm going to teach you. Oh, I'm going to teach you. And how I will teach you, my girl!"

She took her chewing gum out of her mouth. "Why does she in-ti-mi-date me so?" she asked, looking for a place to put her gum.

"Give it here," he said and put it into his mouth.

They walked down the stairs from the back veranda to the cellar. He found the stuff and pulled the door shut.

The backyard was big. The leaves lay scattered by the wind, the brittle layer crunching under their feet. The water in the pool was still. The filter wasn't working. The water in the corners was slimy, there were leaves stuck there. The surface of the water had the shine of green slime, like taffeta, olive green.

Does no one come here anymore? What happened to the young people who used to sit around the edge of the pool laughing, their legs dangling in the water, shaking their long hair in the sun?

"Did you have many girlfriends?" she asked teasingly.

"Sort of," he lied. If they hadn't been carrying all that scuba gear he would have grabbed her around the waist and swung her around.

"Where did we go wrong?" asked the woman in the large car that was sliding softly onto the highway. Her voice was high pitched: "If only someone could tell me what we have done wrong."

K. Sello Duiker

Giant

TANEBA WAS KNOWN AS A VILLAGE of friendly people, rustic in their ways. Young virgin girls still wore ceremonial beads around the neck and the elders still upheld the law and passed down traditions. It was a unique village in that its ways were unlike the surrounding villages. There was much mystery and secrecy about the traditions, especially the initiation schools which were an integral part of village life.

To the east of the village there stood a mountain, known as the Sleeping Giant. It was a mysterious mountain about which the elders had strange stories to tell. Occasionally, a boy herding his sheep at the foot of the mountain would disappear, never to be found again.

On the morning of his fifteenth birthday, Menka woke up feeling excited. Fifteen. What made this one so different, was that he suspected that his year of initiation had arrived. It was a big word – initiation. He wasn't sure what it really meant. By tradition, it was forbidden to talk about it to the uninitiated. It was said that a curse would follow any man who ever spoke about it.

Menka had stumbled upon it while the adults spoke one night. He hadn't meant to eavesdrop; it just happened. He had woken up at night and needed to make water. On his way out he overheard Uncle Mati speaking to his father and Uncle Nima. And that big word, they said it. He couldn't hear whether they mentioned his name in the same breath but there was a hushed tone and solemn silence afterwards, as though the adults themselves were taking in the significance of that word. It was Uncle Mati who had said it.

The next day Menka pestered his older cousin Hapi about that word. Why was Uncle Mati so serious after mentioning it? Yes, why was gregarious Uncle Mati who always had a good story to tell so earnest about that word ?

"It is a great thing," cousin Hapi said and pulled a grin, which puzzled Menka even further.

"But this great thing – what is it?" he went on.

"Well, firstly it is an occasion that every man must go through," Hapi explained, a curious smile on his face.

So when Menka woke up that summer morning, he washed his face at the basin as usual, trying not to show his excited anticipation of what would happen. No one had ever spoken of this "occasion". It was taboo. And cousin Hapi had worn a strange, mysterious grin when he mentioned it.

Menka dressed as fast as he could and rushed to the kitchen. There was no one there. He walked around the house looking for his mother, father and two little sisters. Strangely, they were nowhere to be found. Perhaps something was going on at the market. Or they had gone for early prayers. Menka looked down the lonely dirt road leading to a nearby village. There was no one there. He went back inside and prepared himself something to eat: bread with honey and goat's milk. He ate with a good appetite but he wondered about his family. It was his birthday. Surely they could not forget it, he reasoned, concern overshadowing his initial excitement.

After eating, Menka put on his ceremonial belt around his waist. He wore it because his father was a village elder. Then he walked off towards the mountain. He should at least find cousin Hapi here.

In the verdant valley, sheep were lazily grazing. But there was no Hapi. Menka called his cousin by the special name that only he used for him when they were out in the hills together. "Majunka! Majunka!" he yelled. Hapi got this name, which meant "he that smells", by once falling into a pile of cow dung on his way to the market. He was further embarrassed when the village baker refused to serve him because of the offensive smell. "Majunka! Majunka!" the baker had cried, much to Menka's amusement and to cousin Hapi's annoyance.

But where was Majunka now? The hills were quiet except for the nagging bleating of the lambs. Menka walked towards a small cave at the bottom of the valley where they sometimes rested. The first thing he noticed as he neared the cave was a rock covered in a red substance. Menka touched the red and smelled it. It was blood. But whose blood? He became concerned about Majunka. He approached the small cave carefully, measuring each step. There was enough light to see right to the back of the cave even though it was dim.

And then suddenly, without warning, darkness enveloped Menka. He tripped and fell. He was wrapped in a blanket, and anonymous hands were clutching at him roughly. He tried to fight but his attempts were futile. Strong hands held him down and tied some kind of rope around him and the blanket. Then he felt himself being lifted from the ground with great ease, hoisted over a large shoulder.

"Who are you? Where are you taking me? Majunka, is that you?" he protested helplessly.

No one answered. He could not even feel the sun on his skin even though he felt the warmth of the air.

It must be the giant, Menka realised. The giant has kidnapped me, he thought, remembering all the strange stories he'd heard about the sleeping giant. He could feel that they were moving fast. The giant probably took large steps. Menka thought about his family and felt sad and scared. What was happening to his special day? He thought about what he had heard about the "occasion that every man must go through", and a strange fear that he had never known suddenly gripped him.

They walked for a long time till eventually he fell asleep, exhausted by what seemed to be an endless journey. When he woke up it was cold and night-time. He found himself on a patch of ground without a soul in sight. He did not know where he was. And the mysterious giant was nowhere near him. In the dark, the rocks took on strange shapes, of things he had never seen before. He wanted to make a fire but he didn't know where to find fire wood. And what would he eat? The cold was like a sack against his skin. It gave him goose flesh and made him long for the warmth of his bed and his mother's food.

He walked a little further up and started climbing the rocks till he reached the small top. Above him, the silent stars watched and the crescent moon observed the territory. He couldn't recognise the landscape, the rocky hills and thorny bushes. Something scurried beside him. His mind played games with him in the dark. Was it a snake, a quick viper? He decided to climb down again where the rocks provided a natural shelter against the gentle wind.

He closed his eyes and coaxed sleep to come, resisting a small lump in his throat threatening to dissolve into tears. He slept in fits, praying that the sun would bathe everything in light and sense again. The night held too many secrets and fears.

Morning crept in slowly. Menka felt stiff from a bad night's rest, thirsty and confused. He climbed up the rocks again and at the top he looked around. Things looked better in the light but he still couldn't recognise anything. There was no village in sight. He made his way down again and decided to look for water. He went down a narrow valley.

Along one wall of rock water trickled along the surface like blood seeping from a wound. He sucked the water from the rock and it was tasty, earthy. He felt dirty but he ignored this. His stomach was complaining bitterly. He sucked more water from the rock to still his hunger somewhat before he returned up the valley.

If he walked in the direction in which the sun sets, perhaps he would be able to see where he was, he decided. Surrounded by tall grasses, he continued for what seemed like hours. After a while the tall grass cleared into a rocky path with sparse grass. The land was flat. Tall termite hills, forming strange shapes, towered over him. Except for rabbits and djedjes, small furry creatures, he saw no animals.

He was thirsty again, but he couldn't see water anywhere. After a while he gave up. If he returned to where the giant had dumped him, at least there would be water. Fatigued and with a lump in his throat, he turned back. It was dusk when he got there. He went down the narrow valley again for water. He had had nothing to eat the whole day, and the hunger gnawed at him.

Again he had a terrible night's rest. He dreamt he was chased by a bad-tempered goat that insisted on nibbling on his tunic. But at least he woke up with a plan. I have to eat, he told himself. At the rock he wet his face and drank water till he was satisfied. Nearby there was a bush with wild berries of a bright red colour. After all the time he had spent in the wild with Majunka, Menka knew that brightly coloured food didn't always mean it was edible. He walked around and looked for other berries with tamer colouring. He found a bush bearing purple berries which he recognised, pehati berries. He picked as many as he could, making a small pouch in the front of his tunic. When he was done, he went back up to where he had slept. He put the berries in a neat pile on the ground.

Now how do I get some meat? he asked himself. What about those wild rabbits he had seen? They are too quick to pursue on foot, that he realised. He would have to devise a way to catch them. All he knew was that they liked sweet grass. Fortunately, he noticed some sweet grass growing in isolated tufts around him. He could make a trap. There was a dimba tree nearby whose branches were thin and pliable. With nothing to cut he looked for a stone with a sharp edge. He found one and sharpened it against a rock. He cut many branches. At the market he had seen women weaving baskets. He tried to remember how they did it. At first his hands were clumsy and impatient but his persistent hunger forced him to concentrate. The branches scratched him and he cut himself a few times, minor cuts that annoyed him rather than caused pain. After a long while, and with a fair amount of improvisation, he managed to complete a small basket with an opening small enough for a rabbit to walk through. Once inside, the rabbit wouldn't be able to run out again as sharp branches like spikes were on the inside of the opening, ready to poke and injure. He had once seen a bird trap like that and hoped his trap would work with rabbits.

Menka gathered tufts of sweet grass into a pile and placed them enticingly inside the basket. He then placed the trap in a shady spot near a rock. He went back to his spot where he slept and ate his berries. They were tasty and sweet but he didn't eat too much. Too many berries are a recipe for an upset stomach, he remembered Majunka once saying.

He waited a long time before he heard some screaming coming from the trap. Excitedly he rushed there. Much to his surprise, it wasn't a rabbit he had caught but a small djedje. It was struggling to escape and Menka had to act quickly before the djedje gnawed its way through the branches. Lifting the basket carefully, he carried it back to his resting spot. He put it on a slab of rock. Holding a big stone in his hand, he bludgeoned the djedje to death. Then he skinned the small creature with a sharp stone and put the meat through a skewer he had made of a tough branch. The skin he stretched out to dry in the sun. He used two quartz rocks to start a fire over which he roasted the meat slowly. As soon as he started eating, he felt a lot better.

The following days were all passed like that. Not once did Menka see another soul. The only sounds he heard were of small animals, the wind, birds, and eagles screeching overhead as they extended their expansive wingspan in the sky. He built a small shelter from the thin but pliable branches of a dimba tree. His bed was made of wild grasses that had dried in the sun.

At night when owls and nocturnal mice cried, he thought about his family. He missed them. He would just have to find his way home again.

Then one night, he was woken by hands clutching at him. Again he found himself engulfed by a strange darkness as a blanket swallowed him. He protested and fought but the large arms holding him worked deftly. He felt himself being lifted on to what felt like an expansive back. Was his kidnapper the giant again? Menka cried out, asking this, but the giant said nothing. They walked for a long while again. But this time Menka didn't sleep. He stayed vigilant. He wanted to see the face of his kidnapper.

84

It was hot in the blanket. At last the giant stopped. He put Menka on the ground and proceeded to untie the noose carefully. Menka faintly saw big arms attached to a large torso. And then without warning the giant lifted him and threw him up and across. Menka felt himself being catapulted into the air.

A sudden cold splash of water came like a shock to Menka. He let out a shriek and struggled in the water to free himself from the large blanket. When he came up to the surface there was no one in sight. Confused, he swam to the shore. This time he knew where he was. This was the lake where he sometimes came to swim with Majunka. On the other side of the lake he could recognise another village. Home was not far away.

There was a clean tunic beside a log on the grass. Menka examined it in the early morning light and saw that it was one of his own. He was surprised but didn't make too much of it as the last few days had been full of surprises and intrigue. All he thought of now was going home.

He took off his dirty tunic and washed himself in the lake. Strangely, he felt as though someone was watching him as he washed. But who or what it was, he couldn't say.

He dried himself with the dirty tunic and put the clean one on. He started setting out for Taneba, his own village. He had a different feeling about himself. It was as if he had discovered something fearful and mysterious about life. And he felt as though he would have to learn to live with this fear, that it would always be there. Giant men could mysteriously snatch you and dump you in an alien environment and leave you to fend for yourself.

At home he knocked on the door like a stranger. His mother opened.

"Menka, why are you knocking, you silly man? Come in. You left without saying goodbye," his mother bundled him in. "Your father told me that you went to visit cousin Lesha. You could have said something, you know?"

Man? Is that what she said – man? Menka thought.

He was anxious to tell her that he was kidnapped by a giant. That he was in a desolate place with no food and no place to sleep. He wanted to tell her everything but he didn't. At the kitchen table his father and two sisters sat. They were drinking tea. His mother took his old, dirty tunic from him and disappeared into another part of the house.

"Are you hungry?" was all his father said. They looked at each other. Something in his father's eyes told Menka that he knew something about what had happened. But not one of them said anything.

"No, thank you. I just feel tired. I want to sleep," Menka replied.

When his mother came back, Menka told her he was going to lie down for a while.

"But you haven't eaten?" she began to complain.

"Mother, I'm fine. I just want to sleep a bit," he explained.

"Let him sleep, the man says he's tired," his father said. It was strange to hear his father calling him a man. He had never said it before. But it was all he needed to hear for everything to make sense. He understood what had happened to him over the last few days. The occasion, he thought as he went to his room, it happened to me. A smile grew on his face.

He went to bed. Under his pillow, wrapped in the familiar pelt of a djedje, was a knife with an exquisitely crafted handle. He knew it was a valuable gift and he put it away in his cupboard, where his mother would never look.

The next morning, he went to the hills to look for Majunka. He wanted to say so much to him. When they met they embraced as always.

"Lambs are not so different from children, you know," Majunka began before Menka got the first word.

"Why do you say that?"

"Because sometimes when they are not well you have to take them away from their mothers. And you can see the sadness in their eyes. But when you take them back to their mothers they get so excited they sometimes piss themselves," he said, sucking at a blade of grass and hardly looking at Menka.

"I suppose so," Menka said but he knew what Majunka meant. Nothing was mentioned about the occasion.

Majunka turned to Menka and smiled knowingly.

That afternoon after they had herded the sheep into a pen, Majunka did something he had never done before with Menka. They went to the back of the house where there was a small ceremonial quad where the men sat when they gathered. Majunka sat with Menka and drank mogro root beer on ceremonial stools. They talked into the evening about their plans for that summer. Uncle Mati had talked about the chance to go travelling with him. They talked about the village girls who were becoming women and the ones they liked. But it was still too soon to think of courting. They first had to build their own houses.

Menka felt glad to be back in the company of his cousin. He was aware of himself in a different way, the way a tree knows how many leaves are growing on it.

JEANNE GOOSEN

Ben Prins's feet

EVEN AS A CHILD, ONE KNOWS THAT THERE ARE certain things one simply does not blab about at home. And they don't even need to be things that you have done wrong. Somehow it just doesn't feel right to talk about everything you do and everything that happens to you. Maybe you just don't feel like sharing these things with anybody else. Besides, they won't really understand what it is all about and anyway, you don't really always know yourself …

Like the thing with Ben Prins's feet, that I had to scratch in his bedroom on Saturday afternoons while he and his wife were lying on their double bed, reading magazines.

People used to say that Ben Prins wasn't from around these parts. He was too fancy. He spoke English with an accent. My mother said that it was an Oxford accent. My father said he was trying to be grand.

Ben Prins smoked cigars with a stylish flourish. There was gold in his teeth and the frame of his glasses was also gold. He wore a whitish straw hat with a little feather in the band. When he wasn't wearing a hat you could see that every hair was in place, parted in the middle and shining with Brylcream. He walked with a swagger, slightly kicking his one leg out, like a movie star. He permanently had a faint smile on his face – as if something was amusing him. And then there was his car, brand new out of the box, a dark green Henry J. People said that his wife suffered from nerves. She seldom came out of the house. You never met her in a shop or butchery or walking down a road. God alone knows what she did all day inside the house. She wasn't the kind who liked working in the kitchen or doing embroidery. One could sense that.

Sometimes Ben Prins played nostalgic, sentimental and romantic songs from musicals on the piano. Things like "Sweetheart" from *May Time*. "I'll walk with God", "Indian love call", "Ah, sweet mystery of life" and "This is my lovely day".

When he played the piano, all the housewives in the neighbourhood suddenly began watering the geraniums and the begonias on their verandahs. They were silent, listening. When you tried to greet one of them she would ignore you, standing there with a melancholic smile and a faraway look in her eyes. Like she wasn't really there at all.

"That man plays so … with feeling," my own mother said, enraptured.

I think all the neighbourhood women were sort of in love with Ben Prins. When he and his wife got into the Henry J, all dressed up to go and visit, they peeped out the windows. It was a grand thing to see Ben Prins walking ahead of his wife to open the car door for her.

"He's a real gentleman," my mother would say, impressed.

"A real fancy pants," my father would reply, hitting at something with the fly swat.

"Beautiful!" Makkie from across the road would mumble. But her husband would laugh and say: "Why, old Ben Prins is feeding worms to a fish he's already caught."

We children treated Ben Prins and his wife with great veneration and we greeted the couple more respectfully than any other adults in the neighbourhood.

One Saturday afternoon I was pulling out thistles for my rabbit on the little grass patch next to Ben Prins's house when the window of the Prins's house opened. It was Ben Prins himself. He indicated to me that I should come to the front door. I walked around the house where he was waiting for me dressed in his pyjamas and dressing gown. Then he took me by the shoulders and led me through the dark passage into the bedroom where his wife was lying in her underwear. She was reading a *Woman's Own* magazine.

He went to sit next to her on the bed and took off his slippers. He swung his legs onto the bed and asked me whether I would please scratch his feet. His wife didn't even look up at me.

For the next half an hour or so I scratched and scratched and got to know my scratching well. And Ben Prins taught me how. Taught me without saying a single word about how one has to scratch to please, to make and keep someone happy. He taught me by moving his big toe, by stretching his foot forwards, turning it here and there, and also in the way that he lifted his toe or how he rubbed his heel against the duvet.

After a long time and after much concentration Ben Prins suddenly bent his knee and I knew that this was a sign that he had had enough.

He walked with me to the door, bowed slightly and gave me a tickey and then he said: "Next Saturday?"

I nodded my head.

And then the ritual started. Every Saturday I did my duty. Of course, I didn't tell anybody about my foot job at Ben Prins's house. It didn't feel right. Although I wasn't doing anything wrong I didn't know whether my mother would like the idea. But that wasn't the only reason why I kept quiet – I knew that I didn't just scratch Ben Prins's feet for the tickey he gave me afterwards. And I think I was scared that the neighbourhood would like him less if they knew about it. And so I made sure that no one noticed where I vanished to on Saturday afternoons.

My task captivated me and I couldn't explain why. I wanted to do it well and later I picked up all kinds of pieces of glass and things that I thought would be nice to scratch Ben Prins's feet with. After a month I had collected a whole shoebox full of pieces of glass. There was one piece, a dull dark blue one which was blunt on one side for between the toes and bumpy on the other side for the heel – and that piece of blue glass made him close his eyes with pleasure. He sank his head into the pillows and sighed, "Uh-uhmmm-m."

Ben Prins had beautifully shaped feet. He didn't have any calluses or lumps or corns. His feet were pale and narrow with a high arch. The nails were cut short and the toes had no hairs on them. They were the feet of someone who had never done a day's hard work. They reminded me of the feet of the statue of Christ at the convent near our house.

And so I scratched Ben Prins's feet every Saturday – until they moved away.

Funny, but until today I have never told anybody about my foot-scratching Saturdays. I had forgotten about it long ago. Until this morning.

I was on my way to work and at the traffic lights on the main road I saw a whole lot of people. Someone said it was a hijacking and the driver had been shot dead. There was a blanket over the body. And then I saw it – the one foot. It was peeping out from under the blanket. It was a well-shaped foot, pale, narrow and with trimmed toenails. I stared at it, fascinated. And then I remembered. It was a foot like Ben Prins's, one which I had known intimately.

Right then, in one of the flats on the other side of the main road someone began playing a nostalgic song on the piano ...

THOMAS RAPAKGADI

The purse is mine

THE METRO TRAIN PULLED TO A STOP as the rays of the morning sun gleamed across the township. Pulling his woollen cap over his dreadlocks, Akufani shuffled aside to let Vusi hop in.

"Well, I won't dump Thandi just because she's a gold-digger," Akufani continued and pulled up his baggy turn-up trousers as he took a seat. "I'll keep stealing to satisfy her lust for money."

"Bah!" grunted Vusi. "For how long will we be able to make a living out of robbing people?"

Akufani groaned. He squinted at Vusi, hating the question. "For as long as people have excess cash to be relieved of." He spoke softly, in case the conversation might be picked up by other passengers at the end of the coach. "Mind you, if you develop rubber knees, you won't have your girl for much longer. Believe me, these days girls want to be impressed. Nowadays money can buy true love, my bra," he added mockingly.

Vusi nodded quietly. "Today is as good as any other to go hunting for a job," he ventured. "A real job."

But Akufani deftly turned the talk around to the importance of "fast bucks" to maintain materialistic girlfriends. The conversation continued in this vein until they hopped out at Park Station. They loitered towards a group of female hawkers and fruit vendors. Shoving his hands into his pockets, Akufani lolled around on the pretext of being a prospective buyer. He nudged Vusi and winked at him to start the job. He frowned deeply when Vusi did not respond. Was Vusi beginning to repent? To betray him?

With a sudden movement Akufani thrust his hand out, grabbing a purse.

"Robbery! He snatched my wallet!" screamed one of the women.

Soon, the women swarmed Akufani. His eyes were wide. "I didn't mug anyone! I didn't do anything wrong. I just reached down to select a few ripe pears," he babbled, breathing hard. "I am innocent, ladies!" His protuberant eyes signalled the urgent need for help, but Vusi was nowhere in sight.

The women's voices joined angrily: "We're fending for our kids, and then such a bloody … don't let him get away!" They attacked him, striking at his head with pointed shoe heels. "Kick him!" one of them screamed.

Fighting like a wounded animal, he tried to resist the women as they clutched at his baggy trousers. In vain, he tried to muscle out. Some of the women held him in a firm grip, while the others struck at him with umbrellas and other weapons of assault, grabbed from their trading tables. Then at last he managed to pull away from the women and slip through the human circle, dropping his woollen cap as he fled. He gathered more speed. His dreadlocks spread out wildly about his head.

The women took after him in hot pursuit. They hurled tomatoes and fruit at him, which hit his grey blazer with a splat. "Catch that thief!" bawled the woman on whose crop of oranges Akufani had trampled when he fled.

"Please, mothers, spare my life!" he wailed, bending down to pull on a shoe which had slipped off, leaving his one heel completely bare. He saw the women close behind him and quickly pulled off the shoe, clutching it as he continued to run. With renewed speed he fled before the women's ugly wrath.

By now they weren't shouting anymore, but he could still hear their feet rattling on the pavement.

Akufani gasped and coughed in exhaustion. How could he avoid them cornering him in the dead-end at B & C Restaurant? Then he heard a man's voice urging the bystanders on, "Come on, we're all tired of these criminals, let's get him!" Smelling death, Akufani sped off in the opposite direction, summoning up all his energy.

He flicked around the corner at Grey and Loveday Streets, crossed busy Commissioner Street. He had managed to shake them off! He was out of their sight. At last.

Still exhausted, Akufani panted as he slumped onto the kerb. He took off the blazer, put on the shoe. "Phew! That was close! At least no serious injuries. And no policeman had joined in the chase," he thought, very relieved, and wiped his face. But where was Vusi?

I need some refreshment, Akufani thought, jamming a long, slim cigar into his mouth. "It really doesn't seem to be my day today," he sighed.

Then Akufani spotted a thin, short, elderly man, hobbling along on his cane. Could this be another harvest for the beloved girlfriend back home? Akufani flicked the ash off his cigar. Instead of drawing at it again, he extinguished it and slipped it into his pocket. Once again, Akufani squinted at the man. He studied him carefully and noticed the bulging left pocket of his jacket.

This time Akufani wanted to go about it perfectly. He wanted to avoid another brawl. He glanced around as the old man rattled past him, leaning on his battered stick. Akufani tiptoed behind the man. Then he whisked a bulky purse from the old man's lower coat pocket.

Almost immediately, Akufani felt a firm grab on the nape. Police! One of the two policemen seized him by the belt. "Move!" he shouted. "Let's get to the old man before he crosses the street!" He shoved Akufani along, grabbing the purse from him first.

Akufani spluttered, protested fiercely as they traced the old man. "Do you want to donate my purse to the old man? The purse is mine!"

"Not so. We saw you stealing it from the man."

They caught up with the old man in Jeppe Street. The man took his long brown wooden pipe from his hollow mouth. He craned his thin, scraggy neck, and peered closely at the purse. "I'm sorry, gentlemen. I've never seen this purse before," he said. He turned, pointed his staff at the pavement and leaned on it as he went along his way.

Akufani beamed a smile of triumph. "I told you that the purse was mine."

"But, we're sure we saw you pinching something from the old man's pocket. It might be that his eyes are too old to identify colours, or his mind too senile to remember all his belongings," said one of the policemen. They led him away, towards the caravan charge office parked nearby.

"Why should I accompany you? You don't even have a complaint against me! You know nothing about me," Akufani protested wildly. "You wanted to give away my purse to your old man. And now ... I'm sorry, gentlemen. I'm sorry." He kicked at the pavement as the policemen seized his hands and dragged him away.

At the charge office, the police opened the bulging purse. Thirty packets of cocaine and ten of dagga splattered onto the counter.

There was complete silence. Then the policeman behind the counter squinted at Akufani with a wry, mocking smile.

"So?"

BUNTU SIWISA

The Big Bad Wolf

"SON! SON! *WEH, NYANA!*" Ma always calls me in that specific business-like tone whenever she's about to send me on some errand while I'm lounging about.

"Ma! I'm over here, Ma."

"Get your black jacket, the one with the black hood, and take these to your grandmother right across the woods. Oh! Watch out for the Big Bad Wolf now."

"Oh, Ma, I know that. How often should you remind me of the horror of the Big Bad Wolf? I'm an old boy now, a man of the family, *in-dod' omzi.*"

"Oh, wasn't your father a man, indod' omzi? Hmm? And where is your father now? Wasn't he eaten up by the Big Bad Wolf? It's not safe outside any more these days. On his way back from work, a simple drive from work, and he was eaten up by the Big Bad Wolf, just like that. Wasn't your brother a man, indod' omzi? Hmm? Where is your brother? Gobbled up by the Big Bad Wolf. Do you all have to end up in the stomach of the Big Bad Wolf? Do all the men in this house have to be snatched from me by that bastard, the Big Bad Wolf? You and I are the only ones left in this house. You are the only one I'm left with now. My only son, my man. You cannot afford to end up in that horrible stomach of the Big Bad Wolf. Do you get that?"

"Relax, Ma, relax."

"Now take this basket with the food and medicine supplies to your grandmother. She's very sick, you know, bedridden. Take the car, and, oh, don't forget your jacket, the one with the black hood."

"Stop it, Ma ..."

"It's very cold outside, you know. Now take the black hooded jacket and hop along. Oh! And keep an eye open for the Big Bad Wolf."

The Big Bad Wolf? What, have you never heard or got unfortunately acquainted with, the Big Bad Wolf? Oh, come on, now. You don't know about the Beast, the Beast and a Half, the One and Only Beast, the Beast that Horrifies? He has an uncannily familiar face that never fails to appear on our television screens every now and again, with mammoth white WANTED letters ever circling his head. They seem to think that we will find it difficult to recognise him on television, so they turn his face left and right to showcase all his features that spell nothing but the B, I, G, B, A, D, W, O, L, F. He has an unbecoming fetish for accessing our dwellings and, at howling point, take our TVs, video machines, jewellery, and everything that rambles with rands. When overcome by a gentlewolfish mood, he scrapes the decency and the courtesy together to tiptoe into our homes in our absence or while we are asleep, in order to commit his untoward missions. He is the one that snatches our cars on the road at growling point. He has a very strong, long, hairy and disgustingly reputed hand for grabbing away purses. Nowadays, he has been so ravenously captivated by MTN's "The Better Connection" call that he never misses a cellular phone resting nonchalantly on a hapless human lap. Every full moon, he is driven to gigantic missions of licking clean banks and all the other establishments glaringly gleaming with gold and all that glitters. He harbours a brutal fondness for the fairer sex. All of that, and all of that, spells nothing but the B, I, G, B, A, D, W, O, L, F. Delight is an exiled sentiment to those whose paths crossed with his fatal paws. Delight is a sentiment that skips the heart with an exit permit to those who so unfortunately have brushed shoulders with him. For he is the Beast, the Beast and a Half, the One and Only Beast, the Beast that Horrifies.

It is against him whom my mother warned. On my way to my bedridden grandmother across the woods, I have to keep a vigilant eye for the Big Bad Wolf, lest I be destined for his stomach. That is what she is going on about.

"Can you please step out of the car, Sir?"

A road block? What is it now?

"Good evening, Sir."

"Good evening."

"Can you please show us your driver's licence?"

"Sure, here it is."

"What is your name, Sir?"

"Ndoda."

"Ndoda who?"

"Ndoda Mnyama."

"Whose car is this?"

Here it goes, the usual story. "Excuse me, Sir, officer, why didn't you stop *that* driver too?"

No answer.

Why *didn't* he stop that white driver?

"Whose car is this? Answer the question."

I suppose my kind, my species, my peculiar species, is not lawfully supposed to drive the latest BMW model. A degree holder, a doctor, an engineer, a lawyer, a high-powered entrepreneur – the bottom line is, as long as I bear an impeccable resemblance to the worst side of my species, I am not supposed to drive a sophisticated car like this. Even though I am definitely umpteen times more schooled than these white policemen.

"Whose car is this?"

"The thing is ..."

"Whose car is this?"

"My mother's."

"Oh, yes, sure, right. What's in the basket?"

"But ..." Dammit! "What have I done now? What the hell ... Why are you handcuffing me? There's only food and medicine supplies in that basket for my sick grandmother who lives right across the woods."

"You are coming with us to the police station. You'll explain everything there."

"Sorry about that. We thought you were the Big Bad Wolf. He has hijacked a BMW like this and gunned down the driver, a middle-aged white woman."

That was how the powers that be explained their treatment of me. Dammit! Does the Big Bad Wolf have a university degree, does it hide its head every night in the suburbs, does it dress up like me? "We thought you were the Big Bad Wolf ... " To what length and breadth do I have to go to prove that the Big Bad Wolf's teeth could easily snap into my flesh as well? That I could be a victim as much as anybody else ...

For some strange reason that only a mechanic's mind would be able to puzzle out, my car gets stuck right after this incident, and here I am traversing the woods with this basket. It is getting dark fast and I can hardly see a thing. Only a wolf's night-befriended eye can ease through such woods. I've only been to these woods once; you can almost call me a lost soul around here. But there's hope. There's somebody out there, coming my way. It's a white girl. Maybe I can approach her to help me.

"No! No! Leave me alone. Please, leave me alone," she cries out and stomps away.

"Do not fear! Do not fear!" I plead with her. "I won't harm you! Can you please show me the way to my sick grandmother's place. I have to give her this basket with food and medicine supplies."

"You'll rape me. You'll beat me up. You'll bullet me down. You'll murder me. You are the Big Bad Wolf. You'll eat me up."

"No! No! I'm no rapist. I am decent and law-abiding. I'm no Big Bad Wolf, no Big Bad Wolf holds a university degree and puts on a Christian Dior shirt sprinkled with Coco Chanel cologne."

I prostrate myself in front of her.

But she is not convinced. "You are the Big Bad Wolf. And you will gobble me up."

She runs away, leaving me behind. Like all the lambs in the woods, she has seen many Big Bad Wolves, and they all look like me. Dammit! How do I have to prove to them that I am not the Big Bad Wolf? How can I prove to my fellow human beings that I will not brutally take what's not mine? What do I have to do to prove to the woman that I am not the one who will rape her?

Look, here I am, like all the lambs in the woods, besides myself with fear that the wolf will mug my soul.

Oh, my God! Here he is. There he is. That's him. That's exactly him. The Big Bad Wolf! No figment of doubt at all. He bears the scorchingly sun-grilled skin that all Big Bad Wolves have. No doubt, no shadow of a doubt at all. He has the dagga-darkened thick lips characteristic of all the Big Bad Wolves. No doubt, no inkling of doubt at all. He brandishes about his appendage that says he is the he-wolf, the whole he-wolf, and nothing but the he-wolf. No doubt, no doubt at all.

That's definitely *him*. Okay, calm down now. They say that wolves only attack those who appear to fear them. Let me speak his language.

"Heita."

"Hola! Hola!"

"Moja, wat sê?"

"Sharp, sharp."

"Mfowethu, where are you headed?"

"To my grandmother's place, right across the woods."

"Check here, broer, I think I should warn you. You'd better take that way. This one will lead you straight into the Big Bad Wolf's stomach."

"Oh!"

"Yes. If you don't want to end up in the stomach of the Big Bad Wolf, be advised to take the other way."

"Oh!"

"Now, hop along, Little Black Riding Hood, and watch out for the Big Bad Wolf."

Unbelievable! Unfathomable! Who is the Big Bad Wolf? If he appears neither in Christian Dior shirts sprinkled with Coco Chanel colognes, nor in dirty blue workers' overalls and striped golf T-shirts with All Star takkies and with a spottedly shaved head, then who *is* the Big Bad Wolf?

At last ...

"Hello, Grandma."

"Hello, son of my son."

"Grandma, why is your voice so hoarse?"

"Oh, son of my son, isn't it because of this sickness of the senile that never ceases to sjambok me?"

"Grandma, why is your chest so broad?"

"Oh, son of my son, isn't it because of these burdens of wood that I have to shoulder through these woods?"

"Grandma, why are your hands so huge, thick and calloused?"

"Oh, son of my son, isn't it these fires that I have to set and quell to keep these old bones warm?"

"Grandma, why are your teeth so long, yellow, dirty and dark?"

"Ah, son of my son! Why all these questions? I am an old woman now. I am too old. That is why I have changed so much."

Phew! For a moment I thought that the Big Bad Wolf had gobbled up Granny, and was masquerading as her. Where is the Big Bad Wolf then? What does he look like? Who is the Big Bad Wolf? Am I the Big Bad Wolf? But then, I do not howl, nor bite, nor horrify. Who is the Big Bad Wolf then? Is he then after all the one I met in the woods? But neither does he howl, bite or horrify ...

Who is the Big Bad Wolf? Is there such a creature? If there is one, if I am one, if he in the woods is the one, then please God ... bless all the Big Bad Wolves and keep them from extinction.

BEVERLEY JANSEN

They didn't even print his name

CHANTELLE WAS THE FIRST TO ARRIVE. As she walked into the room, she glanced at the pictures on the wall. They were all crudely drawn. Pre-primary art. She eyed the brightly coloured pictures and wondered why small children drew such silly pictures. She focused on one of them: a man with no hands, large feet and one eye in the middle of his forehead. Her eyes darted to the next picture: a big woman with huge hands and a smiling face like the sun. Why were all the men in the picture so small compared to the women? She glanced at her watch. Seven o'clock. Would she be the only fool turning up for this meeting? It was always a worry getting home after dark, if no one else from your own neighbourhood came. But surely, at least Verna would have to turn up.

She pulled a chair towards her. It was one of those small pre-school chairs. A bright yellow one. She stretched her long legs in front of her. The door opened wider. Chantelle recognised Clivie. She had last seen him at such close quarters when they were both in standard eight. She noticed the gold studs in both his ears immediately. His hands were deep in his pockets. This made his jeans sit well below his hips. Chantelle fought off a grin – if he were not wearing a thick padded jacket, she was sure she would see parts of his anatomy she had rather not.

Clivie didn't smile at her. Only asked, "Hoesit, Girlie, are you here for the meeting?"

She hated that nickname, but decided against antagonising him.

She pursed her lips, trying to look nonchalant. "Ja, I'm just coming to listen, I don't know what I can do about this business."

She noticed that two of his front teeth were missing. To think he had such beautiful white teeth when he was younger. He had a fresh scar under his left eye. Must be from the weekend's fight. When is it going to stop? she sighed inwardly. When one of them dies? This was the ghetto. You're born without much fanfare, you sort of live for a while and if you are male, you die young and violently. Unless of course you manage to get out in time.

Clivie looked straight at her and she felt uncomfortable. She hoped he couldn't guess what was going through her head.

He began humming a tune to cover his own awkwardness. "Verna is mos lekker mal if she thinks we can break this thing."

She didn't answer him. Didn't think it would help to repeat what Mummy always said to her, words that gave her hope on occasions like this one: "My child, where there's a will there's a way."

Clivie and Chantelle sat in silence for another while. Her eyes travelled to the storybook characters on the wall. His rested on the colourful buttons, sucker sticks and cleanly washed peach pips in the plastic tray on the small wooden table. Then there was raucous laughter outside the door, and in the others walked, one by one.

Donnie was first. He looked even smaller and thinner than usual. But then, size never mattered here. He had built up a reputation as a fearless fighter. Chantelle smiled at him in recognition. He nodded back.

Behind him walked Sandra, her face flushed from the walk. She had always had a bit of a weight problem. Tonight she looked like a stuffed teddy in her red fun-fur jacket. She was the first to talk. "Am I late?"

Chantelle looked at her watch and shook her head.

"It's my laaitie, he didn't want to sleep. I think he's cutting teeth," explained Sandra importantly.

"Nou, brêk djy?" Clivie asked. "Djy's self nog 'n laaitie."

Sandra didn't reply. She knew better.

Chantelle studied each face as they were cracking jokes about the weekend's clash. She remembered not to stare too long at each face. They hated being stared at.

The whole lot turned up. All the members of the Bubblegum Boys. They had fought almost the entire weekend. The Bubblegum Boys versus the Terror Triggers. No one could stop them. Not their mothers, nor their fathers, not even the local police. They feared or respected no one. They ran at each other with screwdrivers, broken bottles and pocket knives. Some say it was Donnie who first fired a shot in the air and started it off. It was a miracle no one had died. Donnie's mother, Antie Mien, wept aloud and fainted from the stress; small children hid under beds. Most of the windows of Rosemore Court were smashed. The council will refuse to fix them, Chantelle thought. The people will first have to pay. Brother Jonathan of the Full Gospel Church prayed aloud, but they continued hacking at each other. It was only when police reinforcements arrived from Bishop Lavis that they stopped. Now they knew they were outnumbered. They left the courtyard badly battered, stabbed, beaten and gouged. They carried their wounds like badges of honour. On getting into the police van, or the hoenderhok, as it is known, Donnie directed a barrage of vile words at everyone else's mother, including Brother Jonathan's.

Chantelle shuddered when she thought of the weekend. Not that she feared any of these guys. They had all started school together at Duinefontein Primary. They had all stood in the same line for barley soup and sang in the school choir.

Now they all sat in this tiny room, which smelled of baby powder, camphor cream and floor polish. Tonight they were going to talk about bringing peace to their community, about changing their lives. About hope. Verna, the social worker, had pleaded with them for some time to talk. No one minded Verna – she was one of them. She also lived in the Skurwe Flats. The only difference between them and her was that she had finished high school and had gone even further. She had the guts to study at the university in Bellville. Verna didn't turn up her nose at anybody. She led those who had too much to drink to the safety of their homes and tried to get the younger people to believe in themselves.

Verna came in last. She pulled a little chair out from a corner and joined the circle. "Ouens, this nonsense must stop. Someone is going to die. Donnie, your mother is weeping her eyes out. It is not fair, man. We're in the new South Africa."

They all sat with downcast eyes. Chantelle was the only one who looked back at Verna, but her mind was far away, with Donnie's mother's public conversion at the tent next to the sports field some years ago. She can remember clearly how Antie Mien prayed for Donnie.

Sandra was the first to speak. She held her head at an angle and looked directly at Donnie. "I want a better life for my laaitie. I want him to be a somebody, not a nobody. We must cool it." All the boys stared at her. That made her wilt and she smiled apologetically, not daring to continue. She had learned at home that it didn't pay for a woman to say too much.

Donnie pushed his cap back. His right eye was still blue and swollen. He had a bandage around his left hand. "I don't care anymore … I can maar bloody die," he spat. "I don't care, because no one else does." He removed his cap and placed it neatly on his knee. "Do our parents care?

100

Do the politicians who promised us heaven on earth care? Do the ministers care? I sometimes wonder if God cares."

Chantelle tensed. She didn't like this kind of talk. It always led to trouble. She could see the others becoming more worked up. They were nodding in agreement.

Donnie continued louder than before. "Look at this place! We're living like rats, twenty in a house. Take a look outside at the plastic bags, beer bottles and other gemors lying all over the place." He paused for dramatic effect. "And do you know what … no one cares a damn!"

Verna looked around to give someone else a chance to speak. She noticed Chantelle's hand up and nodded gratefully.

"You're right, Donnie, this place stinks," Chantelle said with a sharpness that surprised herself.

Everyone laughed because they thought she meant it literally. She ignored the laughter. "We must do something ourselves. Make a united effort. March to the police station to complain." She waited for a response. This time there was none. "Or to the council office." There was still no response from the others. Just an uneasy silence.

Verna searched all the faces for support for Chantelle's idea but there was none. Then Clivie, who had been silent all this time, raised his hand. Verna nodded in his direction. He said that he agreed with Chantelle, that they should stand up for themselves. "It's time for us to do something that would make everyone proud of us." Donnie looked at his fellow urban soldier as if he were mad. But Clivie was undeterred. "Look, my broer," he said, "we can start by removing the dirt. Let's clean the place up. Let's clean the junk from the walls."

Donnie was about to jump up and give him a taai klap. Has Clivie really gone mad? The township was divided – the graffiti were the territorial markings. It made it easier for the dealers to know their boundaries.

Clivie claimed their attention again by using well-known gangster signs. "Some of us can draw well," he suggested, "why don't we draw some nice pictures on the walls by the sports field and by the schools?"

Sandra looked happy with this suggestion. She had been the artist in their class, Chantelle remembered. One year she had even won the Fairest Cape art prize. Sandra got up, more daring this time, and said that she agreed with Clivie and Chantelle on cleaning up the place, and drawing decent pictures was one way to start.

Donnie seemed to realise that the idea was gaining ground, since his next words indicated that he would throw in his lot with the others. "Ja, nice pictures of the mountain and the sea, why not?" he said with the slightest of sniggers. "But no bloody Donald Duck and Mickey Mouse shit," he added firmly. "That's from America. We're South Africans ... New South Africans," he said, glancing mockingly at Verna. They all laughed. Donnie looked pleased.

The others asked whether they could also throw in a couple of self-portraits just for good measure. Why not, they all agreed.

Chantelle noticed how cautious Verna went about it. She had to keep the momentum. She had to keep their interest. Everyone was excited now. They slapped each other's backs and gave each other the high five. Sandra winked at Clivie and gave the thumbs-up sign.

It was time to move the meeting to another level. They had to start planning. Where was the paint going to come from, Clivie asked. Donnie thought he knew the answer. "Jong, we'll sommer hijack a truck or borrow it from old Levin's in town." The others laughed somewhat unsurely. Verna didn't appreciate the joke. She didn't want any silly ideas put in anybody's head. Finally, the meeting accepted Chantelle's suggestion that Verna should write to local businesses to ask for donations.

Verna seemed satisfied. She would write the letters. But they would have to take the responsibility to recruit more kids for the cause. Before leaving, they all agreed that they would meet at the same time, same place, next week.

Chantelle zipped up her jacket. She moved closer to Clivie. "Can I walk home with you?" He nodded. He seemed pleased that she was asking to walk home with him. The night air was cold. He buttoned up his padded jacket right to the top and pulled his black-and-yellow cap over his eyebrows. They began walking in silence. Chantelle remembered how, when they were still in high school, the two of them used to talk for hours about TV programmes, pop stars and township happenings. But everything had changed.

Chantelle thought of how Mummy had warned her not to have anything to do with the boys in the blokke. She always said they would come to nothing, just like their fathers. She didn't always agree with Mummy. In any case, right now she'd walk with the devil himself, just as long as she didn't have to be alone. Every man, woman and child knew this place was gangster territory.

She needed to make some conversation to make the journey less uncomfortable. "Nice meeting, hey?" she tried.

"Mmm ..." he answered.

"Do you think anyone can really make a difference, Clivie?" she asked this time.

He glanced at her from under the rim of the cap. They walked in silence for another few metres. Then he suddenly said, "People think we're just a lot of gangsters. Some people think we don't have any dreams. But I also want to help my mother to build a house and to put food on the table."

She was surprised to hear him talk like that about his mother. She thought he and his mother were constantly at loggerheads. She never had anything good to say about her son, anyway.

They crossed the street at a lamp post. There was not much light, but as much as you could expect in the ghetto. Suddenly there was a loud thud. Chantelle froze. Figures had erupted from the shadows between two buildings. They were surrounded. Clivie's eyes were wild like a trapped animal's. "Run, Channie, run," he shouted. She hesitated. How could she leave him alone? They were like a pack of wild dogs. There were ten of them. She knew them – Zakie, Pirre, Gertjie and Danie-boy – the Terror Triggers. Feared by young and old alike. Their faces distorted by cruelty and drugs. Then Clivie slumped down on the ground, as limp as a rag doll. She saw the gap Clivie had created for her and she bolted. She never stopped until she pounded on the front door of their flat.

She had collapsed on the cold kitchen floor. Only after Mummy had given her versterkdruppels, could she tell her what had happened. Soon the neighbours were crowding into the tiny kitchen. Each had his or her own version of the attack. Others congregated noisily in front of the block of flats.

They told her that he had been taken to hospital. But he didn't make it to the morning. Antie Mien said he died on the stroke of midnight. Brother Jonathan said something about living by the sword and dying by the sword. Chantelle didn't or couldn't concentrate any more. Didn't wish to remember Clivie's stricken face. She wished only to remember the meeting. There *had* to be a way to work with Verna to find the peace in which Clivie had begun to believe. They had to, for his sake.

The next day it was in the paper. A gang-related incident, they said it was. They didn't even print his name.

Just another gangster who died violently on a cold night in a dusty Cape Flats township street.

Tom Dreyer

The immortality of lobsters

"WHAT GETS ME ABOUT THESE UP-COUNTRY PEOPLE," Lawrence said, eyeing the pram that stood just outside the shadow of a large Coca-Cola umbrella, "what really gets me are these ever-present sunburnt babies." The family relaxing under the red and white dome seemed unaware of the pitiful wailing. "I mean, in this kind of sunshine. It's like some sort of offering."

John and I chuckled, and we both took another swig of beer. We watched as a woman finally got up, lifted the screaming youngster from the pram and applied suntan lotion.

"Red as a lobster," John joked, still propped up on his elbows. He stretched himself out on the warm sand and closed his eyes. "Damn Vaalies are all the same."

"Could someone please explain to me why they have to lug *everything* along to the beach?" Lawrence groaned. "Chairs, tables, cool bags ... I won't be surprised if they have their whole Christmas dinner here tomorrow."

The baby resumed its crying, and I got up and shook the sand from my towel. "Let's go snorkelling," I said.

"The number thirteen spanner, I'm looking for the number thirteen spanner," Lawrence called out, looking back at us over his shoulder. He readjusted his glasses with a greasy finger.

"Unlucky number," John mumbled from inside the tent, launching a playful kick at me. I was squatting just outside the tent, rummaging in the tool bag. "Ralph ..." he added after a moment's silence. Something in his voice made me lift the flap of the tent and peer inside.

My eyes, accustomed to the glare of the sunlight, could make out only the gleaming rim of an Amstel can. It took some time before John came into focus. "I thought of something interesting this afternoon," he said, "something I heard years ago ..."

I was well aware how John could get carried away by a story; yet I listened.

"When I was in standard eight or nine, an old university buddy of my dad went crayfish trapping with us one Saturday. Uncle Patrick something – he was a priest, a Roman Catholic. I remember how intently he looked at the lobsters flapping about on the bottom of the boat. Later he put out a hand to touch one of their wriggling legs, and whispered something about the immortality of lobsters."

"The *what*?"

"Never mind, I found it strange too. It seems this was an issue the Catholics had debated at some time during the Middle Ages."

"It sounds absurd!"

"Yes, man, but things were different back then. Besides, I can't quite remember what the man said. And it's not important either. I wanted to say: this afternoon, when we went snorkelling, I thought of a way in which the phrase does make sense ..."

John was interrupted by the drawn-out blare of a motorcycle horn. "Could I have that lousy spanner now!" Lawrence bellowed.

After a final adjustment to the Yamaha, Lawrence's fingers caressed the orange flames emblazoned on the petrol tank. He handed the spanner back to me and dropped a superfluous little screw onto my outstretched hand. As he leapt into the saddle, the sunlight flashed on the lenses of his spectacles. I remember thinking that John should have been the one wearing glasses. His nose was forever buried in a book, but Lawrence was the one who looked life straight in the eye. He gave us a two-finger salute, and then, with a final snarl of the four-stroke engine, he was on his way. I watched as the motorbike grew smaller on the smouldering tarmac, then disappeared down the beach road on the edge of town.

Later, much later, I watched the cross on the side of the ambulance, the red strobe light that brushed soundlessly past the faces of the on-lookers. A paramedic touched my shoulder and his lips moved, but I didn't hear what he was saying. I think it was John who helped me get in the back of the ambulance. There was an oxygen mask strapped to Lawrence's face and his right leg trembled slightly.

"Must have skidded on the kelp," the paramedic remarked. I closed my fingers in a fist and felt the sharp profile of the screw that I was still clutching in my hand.

Fluorescent light pervaded the waiting room. The walls were horribly white, and a nurse gave John and myself each a tablet to swallow. There was a tiny Christmas tree in the corner. An electric cable sprouted from it, and ran in loops across the floor. A portable fan slowly swivelled its head from left to right, disturbing the decorations on the tree. I glanced at John, but his gaze was fixed on a sobbing woman and the pale baby on her lap.

My tongue was too dry to speak; later John broke the silence.

"You remember this afternoon, when we went snorkelling," he said, "I was the first to come out. While I waited for you guys, I looked at the three lobsters I had caught. They looked exactly alike; there was no telling them apart. Later I got to thinking about what the priest had said that day ... and that's when I got the idea.

"It's as if there *are* no individual lobsters, as though they are all part of a larger entity, of the *idea* lobster. When one dies, it doesn't matter, because the idea lives on – and in this sense they *are* immortal."

I heard the woman speaking softly to the baby. I saw the lights of the Christmas tree flicker. "I don't know," I said.

Hours passed before the door was pushed open and a doctor entered. His face was grim.

I felt a chill wind sweep across the deserted beach. I felt the world slowly shift beneath my feet. I saw the priest leaning over and picking up one of the crayfish on the bottom of the boat, before lifting it over the side and dropping it into the shimmering blue water.

FRANÇOIS BLOEMHOF

Tupperware

SANDRA STOOD BEHIND THE TREES for a moment to gather courage. What if she got caught?

It was two o'clock in the morning.

By the light of the street lamp the Nels' house looked pale, like Feta cheese. When she had been here earlier, ten hours ago, it looked less imposing.

Do I really have to go in? she wondered. But she had to – otherwise Juan would never be himself again.

The past six months with him had been so good. They had been to the movies, to the Waterfront, gone eating out together …

But then Tricia came to President High School, from Tygerberg High. Immediately all the guys went crazy over her. Must be because she looks so much like Britney Spears, those girls who lost their boyfriends consoled themselves.

And then this morning at school, Juan said: "Sandra, I can't go out with you tomorrow night."

"That's fine, how about Saturday night?"

He blushed uncomfortably. "We can't go out any more. I'm sorry."

Minutes later, when Sandra saw the laughter in Tricia's witch eyes, she knew.

"Come visit me at my house this afternoon," Tricia said. It was the first time she had ever invited any of her classmates home. It was a horrible visit. Sandra realised the only reason she had been invited was so that Tricia could enjoy her misery. Tricia's room smelt of herbs and she kept on stroking a Siamese cat. On the wall she had stuck a poster with strange symbols.

Looks like I was quite right to call her a witch, Sandra thought.

"I bought this dress last December in Paris," Tricia said lightly. "Don't you think the shops there are wonderful?"

"I wouldn't know." Then only Sandra noticed the big heavy box in front of the window. "What's in there?" she wanted to know.

She could see Tricia flinch.

"Leave it alone!" Tricia quickly stepped between Sandra and the wooden box.

And then Sandra knew what had happened to Juan.

And here she was, back at the Nels' house, standing at the kitchen door so scared that she could hardly breathe. But she had to do it. She took a hairpin from her pocket and fiddled with the lock. She used to be good at this when she was in primary school.

Concentrate now. It was nearly open. It won't open. It opened!

The lock gave a click and she carefully pushed open the door. The house was quiet. Her heart gave a jolt as she saw a shape on the kitchen table but it was only the Siamese cat, glaring at her, his eyes like moist stars. Sandra carefully squeezed past him and looked back. He hadn't moved.

Quietly she went up the stairs. As long as they don't creak, she thought. She reached Tricia's bedroom door. It was ajar. Her heart was pounding. Any moment now something could jump from out of a corner. Slowly she pushed the door open. Moonlight filled the room. She could see Tricia lying on her back, her hair curling like branches around her head. She was breathing evenly.

Sandra crept into the room, which smelled even stronger of herbs than earlier today. Suddenly she felt her nose tickle and she had to sneeze. Panic-struck, she somehow managed to suppress the explosion.

She walked up to the wooden chest. The lid was heavy – please don't creak, she thought anxiously. On top of some rags she could see something … the light was bad and she had to scrunch up her eyes to see better – yes, there they were, six fresh hearts, Tricia's latest harvest.

How would she know which one belonged to Juan?

She touched the first heart. It was beating warmly, but it didn't make her feel any different. It couldn't be his. No this one either.

And then she touched the third one and suddenly she could remember their first kiss – the first time they ate ice-cream together.

She picked up the heart and put it in the Tupperware container she had brought along. But then, in her rush to get away, she let the lid of the box slip.

At the bang of the lid, Tricia shot upright in her bed, hissing. She threw off the blankets, her hair wild: "You! You ..."

Sandra ran out of the room and down the stairs, almost falling all the way down.

Behind her, Tricia screamed at her. She sounded hysterical, like she was on fire.

Running through the kitchen, Sandra nearly tripped over the cat. Just managing to stay on her feet, she reached the door, the pavement – and then she ran like never before.

The next morning Sandra met Juan at the school gates. "Hello."

"Hello," he looked uncomfortable.

"Won't you come with me?"

When they got to their hiding place amongst the plane trees by the fence where the boys smoke, she said abruptly: "Unbutton your shirt!"

"Why?" he asked, surprised.

"Don't ask any questions."

When he opened his shirt Sandra could see that she had been right all along – there was a slight dent in his chest.

She took the heart out of the Tupperware and pressed it against Juan's chest. The skin opened and she quickly had to pull back her hand. His heart was back where it belonged. The skin stretched smoothly over his chest again.

"What are you doing?" Then his expression suddenly changed. "Phew ..."

"Are you feeling better now?"

"Yes, but –"

"Don't ask any questions." She could see Tricia arriving for school. She didn't look their way. The two guys walking with her were fighting over who should carry her school bag.

"So, are we going out tonight after all?"

"Yes, but there's something else I must cancel first ..." Juan said before he kissed her. It felt just like the kiss that she remembered last night.

"What was the matter with me?" Juan asked, puzzled.

"It's a long story. But it is over now." She put her hand on his chest. She could feel his heart beating. "Don't you worry. From now on I shall take better care of it."

"What do you mean?"

"Oh, nothing."

The bell rang and they rushed to the quad.

What would life be without Tupperware? Sandra wondered.

RITA SWANEPOEL

Skew lids

MANUS ADJUSTED HIS HEAVY body in the easy chair.

"Today's women look at men's bodies and I'm telling you now, Manus, unless you do something about yours, you won't ever get a woman."

Ma was probably getting all these new ideas from watching so much TV. When he looked at pictures of his dad it was clear that Mom didn't think like today's women. Dad himself had been very large. Mom looked quite nice in the picture, but that was then. Her excuse now was that she ate enough for two people. She could never get used to the idea of cooking less food after Dad had died.

When he was with friends, Manus did what the fishermen did – he always spoke about the one that got away. And he was given the sympathy he wanted, because everyone understood that a man needed time before he wanted to be with another woman. But alone in his room he longed for a companion with whom to talk about his day. Someone to hold. Someone he could cook for. That was the one thing he was quite good at.

He had already secretly sent off his particulars to the lonely-hearts column. He never sent a photograph along but he organised a meeting. He believed that once the girl got to know him she would soon realise that he was a pleasant person.

For some reason or another the women never pitched up. Only some seemed to bother to write a letter of apology about how they got married suddenly or how their mother had become seriously ill.

Somewhere he had heard that the women from these columns didn't wear the clothes that they said they would in their letters. They stand and look at the man from somewhere and if he didn't appeal to them, they vanished.

This morning the car had let him down and he had to take the bus to work. For years he had hated walking in town. At home the mirrors were

111

just large enough to prevent him from cutting himself while shaving but in the street there was glass everywhere – car windows, shop windows, mirrors in restaurants. Wherever he looked he saw his reflection waddle towards him. In the city he couldn't help but see himself just as everybody else saw him.

Once he got onto the bus he had to squeeze himself past the filled seats. The last time he had caught a bus it had been far easier, he remembered frustratedly. On the other side of the bus he saw a girl holding her hand against her mouth. He could see the mockery in her eyes. He noticed her friend nudging her. And then the only free seat available was directly in front of them.

His backside spread over the whole breadth of the bench. Behind him he could hear the muffled words: "We will have to go and sit on the other side, otherwise the bus will tilt." He could feel himself blushing. Just because he was fat did they think that he was also deaf?

When he got to the office he looked around to see whether his colleagues were staring at him; he felt so much fatter today. But everybody seemed to be used to seeing him squeeze his large body past the office furniture.

The ride on the bus had left him bruised. He picked up a pen and wrote in his notebook.

Dear Editor

Please allow me the opportunity to give the reader a glimpse into the heart of a fat man. Articles about diets and obesity are mainly aimed at women readers. However, my fat body causes me just as much pain as it would any woman. It is just as painful when people mock a man's body. At the end of the day I try to forget and the next day I act like the clown again – enjoying laughing and eating.

It even hurts when I laugh, because when I look down I can see the fat shake all around me. Every time I laugh I can see it roll over my stomach. But despite the pain I have learnt to laugh at myself.

All this pain would be bearable if only I could find a life partner who could see beyond this body. I am a sensitive guy, precisely because I know what it feels like to be rejected. My ego has been bruised ever since I was a teenager and all the rejection has made me reach for more food. More layers of fat ... more rejection ... more food. But this obsession with food has also turned me into an excellent cook, something that any woman would appreciate.

112

I hope that this letter will give your female readers more empathy with us fat men. We too can offer much to someone who is prepared to look beyond our layers of fat.

Regards
Fatty

Two, three weeks passed. Every morning he bought the newspaper. Every morning the hope that his letter would appear in the newspaper diminished. It was probably too stupid, he thought. But four weeks later, on a Wednesday, it was published and two days later he received a cheque in the mail, accompanied by a short note: *I would like to meet you and chat about this topic. I have lunch at The Food Pot in Long Street every day and sit at table number seventeen.*

The money from the newspaper was a pleasant surprise, but he wondered why the woman wanted to meet him? He hoped she didn't plan on writing an article about him with pictures.

Three days later he could not contain his curiosity any longer. He came to the office wearing his best jacket, shining shoes and his most colourful tie. Some people asked him whether he was going for a job interview and others teasingly asked if he was going on a date. He could hear from the tone of their voices that they found the notion ridiculous.

The closer lunchtime came, the more he seemed to lose courage. The woman was probably feeling sorry for him. The advantage was that he would be able to brag afterwards that a beautiful journalist had taken him out to lunch. That would teach those who seem to think that fat persons can only find skew lids, if any at all.

The restaurant was two blocks away from his office, too close to drive there. The body reflected in the shop windows challenged him to turn back to the office. He wished that the could walk with his eyes closed.

For a few moments he hesitated at the door of the restaurant. Maybe he should have warned her that he would come today, but then again she might have cancelled. He smiled at the waiter and explained that someone was waiting for him.

And then, without knowing which one table number seventeen was, he recognised the woman. Her body was spread over a bench meant for two. She didn't see him as her face was turned away.

His mind flashed a quick message: "Turn around. A man doesn't want to make a spectacle of himself with a woman like this at his side."

MELVIN WHITEBOOI

The girl with the blues in her eyes

THIS MORNING I HAD DECIDED that today I would kill someone – a man. And here I am now, in the late-night train on my way home and here he is too, facing me. It's just the two of us in the empty carriage. He sits there watching me as if he is trying to remember where he has seen me before. I pretend not to notice him staring at me. The train speeds past the stations: Woodstock, Salt River, Koeberg Road, Maitland … Every station takes him closer to his date with destiny and I am the only one who knows about it.

I lean back, close my eyes and think about the event which led up to this.

It was the winter of 1996. I had just dropped off a colleague in Elsies River and lost my way down one of those little side streets. A group of young people stood under a street lamp with a guitar. I drove up to them to ask for directions.

Only once I had stopped right next to them I realised that I had made a terrible mistake. Four of the men pulled out guns and pointed them at me through the window.

"Get out!" one of them shouted. The others surrounded the car. One of them searched me roughly. They took my money and my gun and then they beat me with their fists and kicked me. The others laughed. They must have been drinking beer and smoking dagga. People were watching from their windows but were too scared to do anything to help me.

Then a whole lot of them jumped into my car and drove off with screeching tyres. One of those who had stayed behind pressed his gun into my back and indicated that I should walk towards the clump of dark bushes on the other side of the road. He was big and had ugly scars on his face. He was grinning at his friends. "First I'm gonna have a bit of fun with this one and then kill him," he said, amidst raucous laughter.

114

When we got to the bushes he ordered me abruptly: "Bend over! Pull down your fuckin' pants!"

I immediately realised what he wanted to do to me. Now, I am not a brave person but the next moment I suddenly turned around. He was so completely relaxed that he probably thought that I would never offer any resistance, and as I turned around, I felt how the gun that was pressed against my back, slid away. I started hitting out blindly at him and got him somewhere against his throat. I could hear him trying to catch his breath. "Boys, boys, the pig got away! Look for him and kill him."

They were searching for me noisily, running towards me, but I had jumped over a fence. It was a mistake because there were dogs that started to make a terrible racket.

"That way, boys, that way!"

She looked about eighteen years old to me. A pretty, slender girl with long black hair and large eyes. She was standing in the door of her Wendy house, staring at me.

"Gangsters," I panted. "They are chasing me!"

She looked uncertain. Somewhere the dogs were still barking and I heard some voices calling. The Wendy house was in the backyard of an oldish, large house. The yard was overgrown with long uncut grass.

After what seemed an eternity she said: "Come inside." And then she switched off the light in the small wooden house.

"Get under the bed," she whispered, pulling the blanket down to the ground to hide me, and then she got back into bed. She must have been sleeping already when I knocked on her door.

When I heard the hammering on the door of the Wendy house I immediately knew it was them. Impossible as it may sound, I knew it was them.

"Open up, or we'll kick down this door!" I heard a voice shouting. It was the voice of the man who had forced me into the bushes. Lying under that bed I went stone cold with fear, frightened and speechless. I swear I didn't even breathe.

"For the last time –"

"I'm coming," she said hurriedly, switching on the light and unlocking the door.

It was him.

"Are you alone?" he grinned. "Didn't you see someone run past here?"

"No, I was sleeping."

"He isn't here, boys, go and look somewhere else," he shouted. "I'm coming just now." Then he entered the Wendy house and closed the door behind him, locking it.

I could hear how he tore off her pyjamas and threw her down on the bed, climbing onto her. He was raping her. Roughly. She gave soft, muffled sobs. An eternity seemed to pass. I was completely paralysed, not able to move at all.

Finally he gave a loud groan like an animal and then it was quiet again. I could hear him pull up his fly. He stood at the door for a while: "Don't even think about telling anyone ... otherwise I bring the boys back here," he threatened. And then he vanished into the night.

She lay on the bed, dead quiet. I crawled out and stood next to her. She lay there stiffly, her eyes staring at nothing. Her pyjamas were torn open in the front and I could see the pretty, firm little breasts. Her red panties were hanging loosely around her left ankle. She was sobbing soundlessly. I sat down next to her and held her tightly against me.

It was a big wedding. My parents loved her and she liked them. We went to Mauritius for our honeymoon. It was wonderful. The cool beaches, the white sand and the friendly people were like balm for our souls.

But then at night everything would change. She didn't want me to touch her. She tried, really tried to make love to me. She didn't want to hurt my feelings, but the memory of that night constantly swallowed her up again, like a monster, leaving her chewed up and hysterical.

She would embrace me, her eyes large and dull, crying softly: "Sorry, I am still not all right. Just give me another chance ... just one more chance, please."

But that chance never came.

One morning while I was still lying in bed an upset hotel manager burst into our room.

"The Madame," he stuttered, "the Madame has walked into the sea. They tried to stop her but they couldn't. Her body was washed out eighty meters on. The Madame ..."

Her eyes were staring at me, just like that evening. I pulled her long white dress back over her legs. Poor, poor child, who tried to save *me* once ...

And now I am sitting here, opposite the scumbag who did this to us. He is slouching on his seat, unperturbed, a cigarette dangling from his mouth. Oh, I have been following him for months already. I know at which shebeens he hangs out. I know where he lives, which trains he usually catches, when he takes the late-night train. I know everything about him. I know him almost as well as if I had created him myself.

And tonight I am going to kill him.

I look out the window. Vasco station. The next one will be Elsies River. That is where he will be getting off the train. I will follow him to the subway under the railway tracks and then I will shoot him without saying anything. And that will be the end of this never-ending nightmare.

The train stops at Elsies River. He is the only one who gets off. I stand at the door and wait until the train moves on. Then I jump off. My heart beats loudly as I run down through the subway, keeping my hand close to the pocket of my jacket.

But as I go around the corner I see him waiting for me, cigarette dangling from his mouth and a gun in his hand. He doesn't say anything; he just presses the gun against my head and takes mine from my pocket.

He drops his cigarette and kills it. He grins and says: "I thought I knew you from somewhere. I always knew that we would meet again. Now bend over!"

Allan Kolski Horwitz

Out of the wreckage

I AM A SOLDIER IN AN ARMY. It is night. I am sitting on a bench in front of a locker. Each soldier has a locker. The locker room is on the ground floor of a large white building which is seven storeys high. I am carefully packing my locker with various things.

On the north side of the building there are streets and trees and other buildings. Here, in a quiet side-street, I have parked a brand-new white car. I now place the keys to this car in an empty magazine, which I hide in the locker. I leave the locker room and walk out of the building. I go to an area of desolate, bare earth which lies on the south side. I am very tired. It is time to sleep but there is no bed or any other comfortable surface on which to rest. I have no choice. I lie down on the depleted, dusty earth.

In the dark I am just able to make out two other men lying close to me, one a fellow soldier, the other unknown to me. We acknowledge each other with gestures, but do not speak. I close my eyes.

I am half asleep when I hear a sudden crashing. I open my eyes. The white building is vibrating. The entire top floor shakes violently. Huge chunks of masonry begin raining down, pieces of brickwork, window frames and doors – an avalanche which incredibly falls only onto the bare, parched stretch of land immediately to the south of the building and not onto the green, built-up north.

The downpour intensifies, becomes more threatening. At any moment a piece of falling debris might hit me, even kill me! I begin to panic. Then, within me, a voice says, "Do not move, stay calm, be still. Wait." The hail of objects continues and despite my great fear, I manage to contain myself.

Then the white building collapses. With a single, continuous motion like a wave, it topples over to the north side and, landing with a shattering sound, causes a massive, choking cloud of dust to rise into the air.

Unbelieving, I stagger to my feet. The storm of masonry is over. I am saved!

Suddenly I remember about my locker and the keys of my new car.

I force my way into the ruins of the building, burrowing through the rubble till I reach the locker room. Tossing bricks and pieces of wood aside, I search everywhere, digging frantically.

There it is!

My locker is still intact. I open it and remove the magazine of bullets. The keys are where I had stashed them.

I step out of the building.

The new white car is parked where I left it – gleaming and whole, untouched, ready to drive.

GEORGE WEIDEMAN

Compress

THE AIR-CON HAS PACKED UP and the December wind burns my face. The mountains are treeless. The plains are treeless. We drive and we drive. I don't know when last we have seen a house. A hot wind forces its way through the windows. My old man could at least have chosen a better place to run away to. The speedometer needle slides beyond 140.

"Slower, Joe, you're killing the car."

"What does Ma know about cars?" The day I got my licence I overheard the guy from the Traffic Department say he'd never seen anything like my driving.

Beyond the speeding nose of the car, a crow flies up from a carcass. Probably a rabbit that had gone to meet its maker. In the night.

One of these days I'll be as free as that speck of a crow in the sky. Free from Ma's nagging.

"You never listen, Joey."

I hate it when she calls me Joey. With so many Johans in the family Pa began calling me Joey. When I was still a lightie. I'd rather not think about Pa. Stuff the old man, it's his fault that we're driving out here now.

Namibia. Do people actually live here?

A freak wind – probably from a ravine – tugs at the car.

"Joey!"

I look at her and laugh. The car is a model of German perfection. I just cannot understand why the air-con has packed up. Maybe the gas leaked out or something. Soon after we had left the border post we realised that there wasn't any cool air coming in. I checked that the thermometer was normal. The eleven o'clock news bulletin reported that, unbelievable as it may sound, their correspondent in the South had said that soon after sunrise the temperature was already thirty-six degrees. Yesterday at three o'clock the mercury had apparently hit forty-eight in the shade. Is that all they can talk about in this country? For the umpteenth time I try to find a decent station – in vain. This time there's just a hiss, not even a crackle.

Ma shakes loose her red dress around her thin legs and rattles another cigarette out of the packet. I notice how thin she's become. She struggles with the lighter. Again and again she squeezes it back into the socket.

"Now this bloody thing won't work either."

I take the lighter from her and rub the ball of my thumb where the glow should be. It's cold. I squeeze it back into the socket. It doesn't jump out. I pull it out and give it a shake. Not even a hint of a glow. Ma scratches about in her handbag. Even turns it upside down. But among the little combs and folded tissues and all the other rubbish there is no lighter. Let alone matches. But the photo is there. I know that every now and then she glances at it.

"What do I do now?" There is panic in Ma's voice. She tries the lighter again.

"Ma can stop smoking. This is Ma's chance."

The look she gives me! Shaking, she packs the stuff back into her handbag.

Pa's photo lies on her lap. It's his fault that we find ourselves on this road. I was ten when he disappeared. Without a trace. Early one Saturday morning he packed his fishing gear into the back of the station wagon – a Saturday morning custom. I heard the dog barking excitedly and I lay listening to the drone of the engine until it disappeared into the distance. I never realised that he had loaded in more than just fishing tackle.

The mountains fold away on either side. An unending expanse stretches into the distance. Over the stony plains the heat sweeps as if over a giant stove plate. It's only mad people who can live here. Or drive here. Of the separation business I don't remember much. Maybe the words were harsher, the reproaches more strident than before.

In the distance a figure looms up. A mirage makes it look as if the person is dancing or floating above the tarred road. When the car flashes past, I see that it's a woman with a baby. She makes a feeble gesture, almost like a greeting. Out of the corner of my eye I see a man come running from the veld. In his hand he is swinging something which sparkles in the sun. A bucket? He waves desperately with the other hand. It's not a greeting. A donkey cart stands a short distance from the road. The donkeys' heads hang. They look like statues. I glance at Ma. It looks as if she has dozed off. She has not noticed these people. I'm glad that she's sleeping. She would've told me to stop. And who would want to stop in this scorching heat? In the rear-view mirror I see how the woman turns around, how the man's arms flop down at his sides.

The road is particularly quiet. All of a sudden a crosswind tugs at the car. Ma's head jerks upright.

"Where are we now?" she asks sleepily.

"How should I know?"

"Don't you read the signboards?"

She rubs her eyes, with a shaking hand, pours tepid water into a coffee mug. Swallows two headache tablets.

"And you could at least be a little more pleasant, Joey."

"I didn't say he should run off to this place."

"It's not to say your father ran away. There is such a thing as memory loss too."

I don't know why she wants to lie for him now. First he discards us like you'd discard a bundle of rubbish on a rubbish dump. Then she struggles to get maintenance out of him. Then we hear he's re-married. After that he vanishes. Everybody thought he drowned. Any fool could see that he had staged the thing.

A board flashes past. Ninety kilometres to the next town. Damn! We have to turn off somewhere here. To the right the tarred road leads onto a sand road.

"That's the one. I'm sure that's the one. You passed it, Joey."

"How was I supposed to know?" I slam on the brakes. The tyres screech, the car swerves dangerously. Ma gives me a reproachful look.

"From here there's still a hundred and twenty kilometres to go. That's what the woman said in her letter. From the turn-off. A hundred and twenty ..."

I don't know whether she's repeating it because it sounds so unbelievable. Or because she's thinking about the letter again. There is something desperate in her voice.

The car swerves suddenly. She lets out a shriek and glares at me with big eyes. I have to reduce my speed and tighten my grip on the steering wheel. The loose sand is deceptive. It's not quite the same as a drive on the beach in a beach buggy with your buddies. Dust swirls in through the open windows. Close them and we suffocate in the heat.

"Can't you do something about the dust?"

"I could stop driving."

"You know that's not what I mean. Jesus, Joey, do you think I'm enjoying this?"

122

The day Pa left we thought his car had gone and got stuck somewhere. Or – worse – that he had gone and picked up a hiker. That he had been moered on the head. That night when his food was getting cold on the table, Ma became restless. When the boxing match started on TV, Ma phoned Uncle Wally. Pa was never one to miss a fight. Uncle Wally said Pa was with him; they were going to phone, but they were too busy chatting. Then Pa also spoke with Ma, he said it's over, he's not coming back. Ma phoned family and friends and told them it was all her fault, that they had had a fall-out. You fought day and night, I wanted to shout out, but I was in standard two.

A year or so after he remarried, Pa disappeared. Together with his fishing rod and bait bag, completely, as if a mysterious boat had picked him up and vanished into the blue yonder. That's how his new wife put it in her letter. One Sunday we drove out to his favourite fishing spot, the Big Rocks, with Uncle Wally. The spring tide had long since wiped out all traces. The seagulls flew curiously above us and then flew away. On Pa's birthday we went to place a wreath on the rocks and waited on the hill until the waves came and swept it away. Soon after that, the Court declared Pa officially dead. And now, hardly nine years later, a creased letter arrived, in a primary school handwriting, full of mistakes. The name underneath – not a signature – said the writing belonged to Anna. That was not his second wife's name.

Sybrand is very, very sick, the letter said. He will probably not be able to get up from the sick-bed. He asked her to write to his wife and son and ask them to come and visit him; there was a lot he needed to tell them. At first Ma would not believe it, but Uncle Wally confirmed that the letter was genuine.

"I'll take you there," Uncle Wally offered. But she told him I had my licence. Then Uncle Wally insisted that we take his car. Ma read the letter over and over. We studied road maps. The letter mentioned only the name of the farm, and where we had to turn off.

We've stopped talking about Pa now. We had been doing enough of that, all the time since the letter arrived until this morning. Then the questions dried up. Ma had become quiet at the border post. But the unspoken questions were eating away. All I knew was that my father, whom I last saw in the year I turned ten, was busy dying from a strange, horrible illness. On a strange farm among strange people. In a strange, suffocating wilderness.

I have to brake sharply a couple of times. Gates every five hundred metres or so. Ma insists on opening them. I let her. When it gets dark a piece of wire nicks her dress and blood runs down her leg. "It's a sign," Ma says. Ma and her signs.

"About what?"

"We should never have come. It's useless."

"But we're nearly there."

"I know." That is all she can say. And she sighs.

Something somewhere lets out a terrifying scream. Ma grabs my wrist.

"Maybe a jackal," I say, not sure.

The wide, still darkness swallows us.

The farmhouse with its solitary lantern light hidden among a scattering of trees. On the stoep a woman with unkempt hair.

"I think you're too late," she says.

Ma squeezes past her. The house smells as if it too has stood closed in the heat. Everywhere Ma flings open windows.

The man whose face is hidden deep in the stained pillow is not my father. My father is a big strong man with a can of beer in his hand and his feet on the coffee table in front of the TV. My father is a man who smells of smoke and aftershave lotion, who ties my boxing gloves and sings with the car radio: "I will love you always."

This man's eyes are dull, his face is decrepit and full of sores; his hands are like the pale roots of weeds.

Ma bends over him and calls, "Sybrand! Sybrand!" And later she sits down, clutching at her handbag on her lap. His eyes stare beyond the ceiling; his breathing comes in jerks.

"He just lies there," says the woman, bringing black coffee on a stained tray.

I can't look at him. I look at the flickering of an oil lamp. And at an orange-red flower in a vase.

"Don't you want to go and see what's wrong with the air-con?" Ma says. She has put her hand over Pa's worn-away fingers as if she wants to hide them. I put the lantern on a rock near the car. The yard is desolate. Near the stoep are two tufts of grass; could that be where the flower came from? The wind has subsided; I walk along the footpath around the farm among the scattered bluegums. The path is cut off from the veld by a row of white limestone rocks. Above my head stretches another path that in this bright light looks as if it too has been paved with limestone rocks: the Milky Way.

After the funeral – there were only about eleven people – we drive back. It's still windy and hot. Ma, who looks as if she hasn't been sleeping these past few days, doesn't say a word, except to say that her calf is sore where the wire snagged her. It's swollen badly, and red. It doesn't look good. We make slow progress, because this time I open and close the gates. And then I have to slow down even more: a tiny hurricane swirls from the veld, swerves suddenly along the path towards us, forcing me to stop. Everything is covered by a red dust blanket. Quick! The windows! With the windows rolled closed, the sweat breaks out on us like blobs of grease. The sandstorm shoots grains of gravel onto the car. I can virtually hear how the paint is being scraped off the car. In the rear-view mirror darkness settles as if night has come. I press the button that controls the windows. Nothing happens. I wipe the sweat from my eyebrows. I press again. The windows stay where they are.

"Why don't you open them up?"

"The flipping things don't work." I try again. Nothing happens. We are as tightly sealed in as in a pressure cooker.

"Now what?" Her voice is hoarse. With clammy tissues she wipes the sweat from her face.

"We have to get out before we suffocate. I'll try and see if I can find the problem."

"I thought you checked the other night."

"By lantern light? Ma must be crazy."

I tried yesterday; some or other electrical fault. The nearest garage is about two hundred kilometres away. "Here we just work on the cars ourselves," a man at the funeral told me. "But we don't drive such fancy stuff."

Suddenly I have a crazy idea: the car's brain has ceased up because of the heat. The bonnet doesn't budge when I pull the lever. I get out, slam the door shut, pull it open again.

"What has got into you?" It sounds as if she's talking to Pa, a long time ago. I try getting my fingers into the grooves of the bonnet. Even a crowbar would not have made it move.

With the doors open, a warm wind blows over us. At least it evaporates the sweat. At least one can cool off a little.

"We don't even have water." She holds up the water bottle; there is less than a cupful. "What are we going to do?" I wish she would stop talking. Ma looks out across the plain. I follow her eyes. There are no trees, not even bushes. Only burnt-black tufts of grass. As if it rained here once, a long, long time ago. The only sign of life is a singing telephone line. Like the dust road, the gleaming lines stretch out into the unending distance. The only shadow is here, underneath the car.

I suggest that we sit in the car; the doors are flung open like the wings of a disabled insect. Even though there is no air here, it is more bearable than standing in the sun.

"If it gets cooler, I'll go and find some help."

But where?

By the time the donkey cart appears, Ma's lips are thick with fever, her forehead flooded with pearls of sweat. A red stripe shoots up along her leg. I had been trying to wipe off her cheeks and neck with some damp tissues, but now there is no more water.

The man and the woman speak quickly in their language; it sounds like pebbles against a sheet of zinc.

While the woman makes Ma comfortable and packs out all kinds of ointments from a little box on the cart, I try to talk to the man. He speaks Afrikaans with a peculiar accent, just as quick and easy as his own language. Then his wife calls him. "Xiriri!" she shouts, or that's what it sounds like.

But it is not his name. He explains that it is a plant, an antidote to poison, and that recently a small strip of rain had fallen a few kilometres back.

For the first time in my life I ride on a donkey cart. The man, his heart-shaped face full of wrinkles, asks if we have come from the city, or if we've come to visit. I'm not so sure what I should say. Among the bedding on the cart a bucket shines.

I say: "My father's dead, we've come to bury him."

He gazes silently ahead of him, speaks in his click tongue with his donkeys.

"My daughter too," he says. "We buried her this morning. Something poisonous bit her."

Again I see the woman at the side of the road; the man with the flailing arms.

After we'd spent hours – or that's what it felt like to me – along the sandy bed of a dry river, he speaks again. "If only we'd got some of those leaves in time," he says, "but it's so dry."

Back at the car his wife uses the leaves to make a kind of compress – or that's what she calls it. "This will draw out the nasty stuff," she says, her hand on Ma's forehead.

STIRRO MOFFAT BANDA

Letters from afar

Dear Mama

Brother Zuki was lying to you when he said we were staying in town. Actually, Mama, I can't afford to stay in town. I lost my job, long ago. I was retrenched, you know. What it means is the boss feels shit about you or regrets the day you were employed. Something along those lines. You know, Mama, you are wiser than me. I hope this letter finds you in good shape. Well, Mama, I am doing just fine. I am trying every day to find a job, I am registered at the local labour offices, I go there once a month or even phone in. God will guide me, Mama. I know I will get a job.

My brother Zuki, your elder son, Mama, is a killer, a thief, a rapist, a crook, a swindler, a drug peddler. Don't tell Papa. He will be very, very cross. You know your man, Mama, he might think of coming down here. No, Mama, please don't tell him. Your son, bra Zuki, is a member of the mafia. The mafia is an organised crime syndicate, so your son, your favourite son Zuki, is a mafioso. He sells anything from stolen goods to hijacked cars, drugs, women, you name it. He has been making a lot of money lately. I mean big money. At times he has come home with more than half a million rands. Cash. Blood money.

One of his buddies sold him out and the police came down on him. As I am writing to you, your son Zuki is out on bail of three hundred thousand rands. Your son's lawyer paid the bail money. Cash. One, two and three hundred thousand rands. Cash. Blood money. A lot of money, Mama, a lot of dirty, shit, stinking, bloody money. Mama, your son Zuki is no businessman. I don't stay with your son anymore. He is still in Hillbrow at The Highveld. I don't mean Highveld Stereo, I mean the block of flats in Twist Street. Sorry, Mama, for trying to explain to you in simple terms, I always forget you are wiser than I am.

Recently, bra Zuki shot his friend point-blank and wounded him. I called the police and they called me a liar. Mama, imagine – me a liar. The man was bleeding to death, and he told the cops he shot himself, he wanted to commit suicide and my brother Zuki intervened and in the process the man shot and wounded himself. Mama, your son Zuki laughed the whole night, he threw a party that night. Dear Mama, don't you believe this? I will tell you what, it is the power of the mafia, Mama. You don't double-cross them. Zuki's friend couldn't double-cross my brother, because he was his boss, you see.

The following day, I went in search of alternative accommodation, so here I am in the informal settlement Re gakanegile. The town is so cruel, its inhabitants are cruel, Mama, Hillbrow no more. They stand at street corners, them sisters, them brothers, looking for clients, I mean them prostitutes and pimps, some of them old, others young, very young, I mean, fifteen years, Mama. Some have been brought to town from Maputo, Mozambique, others from further north. All in search of *idayimani, ndalama, shuma, imali* – wealth. It's pitiful. Slave sex trade, some prosper, some get shot by rivals, arrested by the police, get deported, very few manage to break the chains and run away. Mostly they are caught and brought back again.

Life in Hillbrow isn't a bed of roses. Some make it big, some very big, some huge. It's part of life, you see. *Some are born great, some achieve greatness and some have greatness thrust upon them.* Who can blame them? I just can't stand it, remember when you used to say *stay away from criminal elements,* I am doing just that. There are times, Mama, when I feel like coming home to you. But then I remember, I came here to make money, get rich and one day help you to live a happy and peaceful life.

I want to buy you a mansion in Sandton, that's my dream. I don't want to be a bad boy like big brother Zuki. I'm a good boy. I should now be your favourite son, Mama. I must go, Mama, my candle is burning out, only left with a few rands until I get my blue-card cheque in a week's time.

Pass my regards to all friends and relatives.

I will be coming down to the Eastern Cape some time next month.

Your loving son
Bafana

Bafana

I see no need to write the address. You know it anyway. Don't bother replying we don't want to see your face ever again. Thanks for the letter, you did a great job telling us how stupid you are. We had a long chat and you know what? Don't call us your parents again. We thought you left home for greener pastures. Egoli. Gauteng. Jo'burg. Jozi. But all you have done is to become a police sell-out, an informer.

Your brother Zuki is a self-made man, strong willed. All you're good at is destroying his fortune, shame on you. All Zuki is doing is redistributing wealth, that wealth which formerly belonged to the chosen or the lucky few. He steals? No, your brother is not a thief! He just takes without permission or he borrows permanently from the owners and gives to the poor like us. Who do you think you are, questioning the morality of a man like your brother Zuki like that?

You of all people, you who could have been working with your brother, on his side, as his business manager or his financial advisor. Why did you do what you did? You threw your own flesh and blood to the wolves. Where the hell do you think you will ever get the money to buy us a house in Sandton? Your stupidity has no boundaries, boy!

Your brother did us proud, he was the first in this communal lands to go to varsity. You failed your matric three times, passing only with your fourth attempt. Are you jealous of your brother's achievements? Foolish enough not to admire a good thing when you see it? Your brother had done us all proud down here, he had been the first in almost everything, if not everything. What did you do for us as your parents? Nothing, yes, nothing!

If only we could have been proud of you too.

Busisiwe Helen Banda

MARCEL WILLIAMS

On a sunny day in Lavender Hill

THE COURTYARD BETWEEN THE "SKURWE" FLATS was noisy as usual. The Cape sun had already set, yet children still ran around with abandon, shouting and playing. In the dim light three men tinkered separately on their battered cars.

A sleek, athletic figure stole up the stairway. He bent down behind the wooden stair-rail, obscuring himself from the men and children. When he came to flat 17, he tried the door. Unlocked, as he had suspected. Within a flash he was inside. The TV was playing in the front room, but she was not there. He found her in the bedroom. She was too shocked to scream. Without a word he jostled her onto the bed, holding his hand over her mouth. Ace looked through the undrawn window, catching a glimpse of the star-studded sky. He liked the touch of romance it added to the small room with its basic wardrobe, old mat, untidy bookcase and drab curtains.

The woman was tall and slender, but had well-padded breasts, hips and thighs. Her short black hair clung to the edge of her neck and her forehead, some strands now partly veiling her dark, earthy eyes. These feminine qualities excited him. For a long time he had watched her, stalked her. Now she was brought down like a hunted animal, numb with shock. He enjoyed the wild fear in her eyes.

Then, suddenly, she began to struggle desperately. He punched her. She winced in pain. He would wait no longer. He eased his body weight over the woman. He was going to possess her. Now.

The next morning, Ace felt great as he walked the short distance from his flat to his business. Even the Hills have magic in the mornings, he thought as he looked at the sun-drenched world around him. Ace lacked nothing: wine, women and song were his. The Ace of the place, director of the "Association", he did as he pleased in his territory. Never be seen as

130

weak, otherwise all your advantages will evaporate overnight, was his firm belief. This morning, a new business idea was forming in his head: "I'll add the new product Viagra to my merchandise; give it a trendy name. I'll corner the market; locals will line up!"

In the Hills, Ace represented everything sly and twisted. Ace admired cunning and deception. He had raped before and had gotten away with it. Nobody talked. "No witness, no evidence", was his motto. Even where there was evidence, nobody had the courage to testify. Women lived in fear of him. To Ace they were for the taking. "The last one was young and terrified," Ace said to himself. "Her terror has landed her in hospital. But in time, she will come to enjoy me."

Willem sat on the edge of his bed, dejected. He could not sleep. The night's darkness, its chill air magnified his feelings. He did not know where to put his head. Future loneliness loomed before him, mocking him. He still did not want to visit Evie in hospital. He knew people would say he was a coward. He just could not bear to see her. The rot of the event pervaded everything. He was alone in the flat. His small room seemed to taunt him. He hated the area. There was nothing lavender about the Hills.

Willem's plans were shattered. He was to have popped the question, to buy a house, to have had children with Evie. But it was over now; all that was dead now. As spoilt goods, Evie would only be a shadow of her former self. Maybe he would have the courage to visit her tomorrow, he thought.

But first he would do the honourable thing. He put a notebook and pen on the table and started to plan. Tomorrow morning he would leave work for a while and go back to the Hills.

The next day, Willem woke up in the early morning sun. In his inner self he felt strong and resolute. His day of justice had arrived. He dressed for work and ate breakfast with Greg. The cornflakes tasted dead, the coffee flat. Like a robot he went through the motions, pretending that everything was normal.

"Brother, here's my library book, you said you'll hand it in for me when you go to the library for work ... don't forget, or else it will be overdue," said Greg, as Willem stepped out the flat.

"And please pick up the book I reserved – it's called *Drive-by* by Gary Rivlin," Greg shouted after him.

"Ja, sure, I got it!" shouted Willem, already halfway down the stairs.

When he reached his office, he started working feverishly, constantly checking the clock. At 9.30, he got up to run an office errand to the library. He was planning to stretch this trip, giving himself the extra time he needed for his mission. Grabbing Greg's library book and a folded copy of the newspaper he had kept in his drawer the whole morning, Willem dashed out of the building. He ran to the quiet streets of upper Claremont, checking around him for a car he could hot-wire. The old Ford Escort stood as if waiting to be broken into. This was no problem. The car started and he drove off. The fear of being discovered was overwhelming. He eased the Ford into Main Road. Only when he reached the safety of the steady traffic flowing down to Muizenberg, could he wipe the beads of sweat dripping down his face.

The traffic thinned almost immediately after Willem had turned the Escort off busy Main Road towards congested Retreat. From the vantage of the bridge over the Simonstown railway line, the sprawling suburbs of Retreat, Steenberg and Lavender Hill merged into one sea of houses. His body tensed as he drove down familiar Concert Boulevard towards Lavender Hill. Was it madness that had overtaken him? The fine and sunny Cape day did not match his lunacy. He wondered when the owner would discover his missing car and report it. Could he still abandon the plan? No, he had lost too much. His shame would have no end. He must take control. The lethal 9 mm lay inside the folded copy of the *Cape Times*, on top of Greg's library book. As Willem entered the Hills, he toyed with the weapon, just for reassurance. Would his adversary be there, and would he be alone?

He was in the Hills again, familiar Lavender Hill with its long, barrack-like sets of drab grey flats, quaint wooden stair-railings and untidy streets – a distinct working-class neighbourhood. Children played noisily under drying washing, strung from one building to the next. Devoid of trees, vegetation or grass … how did Lavender Hill get such a name? Its residents, driven to the barren, sandy, wind-swept Cape Flats, lived huddled together in small, semi-detached houses and endless parallel sets of grey flats, the "courts". Their homes, dank miserable hovels in winter, dry sun-exposed habitations in summer, were trade-offs for their inheritance. They had come here as the rejected second class through no fault of their own. They, the bastard children of a class-mad society, were force-removed from District Six. The new suburbs on the Kaapse Vlakte were given ridiculously unsuitable names: Lavender Hill, Bonteheuwel, Hanover Park, Heideveld. All this Willem knew; he wore it, he felt it; he was a product, a *klong*, of the Vlakte himself. Even if he now wanted nothing to do with it anymore, because it had been destroying him from inside.

A handful of pedestrians, interspersed along the winding street, completed the serene scene. His eyes pried for one figure and soon latched onto his quarry.

Ace *was* alone.

Heart pounding, blood rushing through his temples, Willem cocked the weapon in his right hand while awkwardly cruising the white Ford along Grindel Avenue. He turned off the radio, struggling to concentrate, with edgy nerves and fear rising like a flood. What if he missed and Ace drew? Ace could fire and what if he hit him, or even caught a car tyre? Then it would be "game over"! He must beat him to the draw.

As he neared the sauntering figure, Willem aimed. He fired one shot. Ace's body jerked, confirming a hit. Willem fired a second. Ace's body jerked again, like a doll. Ace screamed something. Willem could not hear. He heard only his own shouts: "Die, dog, die!", as if the words were coming from somebody else. As he passed in slow motion, Ace was turning, knees buckling under him, facing Willem. For the first time, Willem could see shock and fear in Ace's eyes. Willem counted three, four, with each blast of the gun. In the side-view mirror, Willem saw that Ace was down. He could not believe it. He had killed a man. Incredibly, each bullet was on target. Yet he knew he was a poor shot and lacked practice.

The few pedestrians ran helter-skelter as if he had shot at random. Willem placed the still smouldering gun on Greg's book and folded the newspaper over it again. He increased speed gradually, trying not to attract attention by driving recklessly. He struggled to swallow, his mouth dry.

Somebody was laughing wildly, dementedly. Then he realised it was himself. He was sweating profusely: forehead, neck, under the arms. His shirt clung to his body. His clammy hands gripped the steering wheel firmly. But he was satisfied. He had killed the pig. Surely, Ace could not survive that? But what if had not died immediately? Ace had recognised him. Would he have had time to tell before he died?

Willem looked at his watch. They would begin to miss him at the office, and he still had to dump the borrowed car, preferably in the same spot where he had found it. There was no more time for the library errand; he would have to do that later, think up an excuse why he didn't manage to do it this morning. He folded the gun and Greg's book into the newspaper.

Everything went smoothly. He left the Escort not far from where he had found it earlier that mornning, first looking around to make sure that nobody had seen him. He slipped back into his place at work quietly, hoping nobody would enquire about the library errand.

The afternoon sun, now in the west, was peeping over Constantiaberg, casting huge shadows here and there over the Hills. Hannes Adams sat in his dark-green panel van, feeling troubled. He was parked at an angle at the edge of the courts where he could see all the activity between the flats and hardly be noticed. His surroundings added to his unease. The overcrowded, grey, drab flats loomed before him, inducing a sickening tiredness. The constant blurring of transistors mingled with the excited voices of the playing children. Impatient, he knew he did not need to stay, but he hung on anyway. Perhaps something there would help to settle the matter in another way. He became irritated by the incessant staring of tenants with nothing better to do.

Just when he was going to give up waiting, he was rewarded. There Willem was, returning from work. He walked up the stairs to his first-floor flat, carrying his briefcase; no sign of what he had been up to to-day. Hannes noted his time of arrival, clothing, every detail he needed. Then he turned his car around, towards the road to Muizenberg. He needed to think. Willem has always been one of the few steady Hills guys, Hannes thought by himself. He had completed school, held down a good job, had a steady girlfriend. A Home Boy, he ignored the gangs, and they left him alone. But tonight there was something pathetic about Willem's gaunt figure.

Hannes pulled up at the beach, hoping to draw inspiration from the constantly rolling waves. He needed to soothe his troubled mind. He did not want to reveal the crime that he had witnessed from his flat window. But he knew that the detective branch would soon contact him. There was no avoiding it. The shooting had happened in Hannes's street, virtually in front of his home. If he chose to withhold the information, they would find out anyway. They would never trust him again. He hated this sideline job. Informing made him a low rat. But he needed the money. For dope. Besides, they would never leave him alone now. Worse, they could turn nasty, leak to the locals. He would be lynched by his own people.

He walked along the wet line, dejectedly kicking the sand. Willem wasn't a bad guy, he thought. Was there no other way out? And Ace deserved what he had got. Willem had been treated unfairly, unjustly; his woman had been violated. But the choice was between his own freedom or Willem's. Soothed by the beauty of the scene, Hannes lingered on. Then, like a flash, it came to him: he had found the solution! He would tell them Pagad did it. Willem was safe. Relieved to have saved a good man, Hannes drove home.

Later that afternoon, Sgt Dave Pienaar pulled up in his car. Hannes feared him most. As senior detective at the Steenberg Detective Branch, Pienaar evoked either scorn or vigilance from his colleagues. Apart from his aggression and occasional bouts of violence, his shrewd and cunning mind could pierce through deception when he needed to elicit information. He would soon latch onto something. Hannes knew he would be hard-pressed to conceal what he knew.

"Your brakes need attention," said Hannes, hoping his eyes gave nothing away. Pienaar ignored this. "Well, don't you have something?" he demanded.

"Like what?"

"Like happenings in the Hills."

"Nothing yet, but I'll sniff around … there's a rumour it was Pagad." He would say no more for now.

"You say? … Okay, find more, remember, no dough, no dope … I must go, a stolen vehicle has reappeared in Claremont."

Hannes watched the car pull away. He hated that smugness. He looked around furtively. Nobody seemed to have noticed the brief clandestine meeting.

At home, Willem put the gun safely back in the wall, removing the loose brick behind the painting. He quickly replaced the painting before anybody could surprise him. He switched on the TV. He sat trance-like in front of the flickering screen. But only the riveting images of the morning's events flashed past his eyes. For the first time, Willem could review at leisure what he had done. He had been lucky, he had pulled it off, he had paid back, he had gotten rid of that bastard that ruined his woman. Nobody would know it was him. It had been fairly easy. He knew Ace always walked down Grindel Avenue at about that time, something to do with gangster business. Stealing the car had proved easier than he had thought. He had shot Ace several times. His getaway was clean. It had all worked so neatly. An amateur had pulled off the perfect murder. Nobody knew.

"Willem, have you heard?" asked Greg, walking in, newspaper in hand.

"Heard what?" pretended Willem.

"The gangs killed Ace a while ago."

"Nè? How?"

"Drive-by shooting … that means gang war again."

"Let them kill each other, what do I care?"

"But don't you feel better … for what he did to Evie?"

"Ja, sure, sure."

"You got my library book?"

"Oops! Sorry, I forgot … never mind, I'll phone for an extension."

"Okay, fine."

Willem reached out for the folded newspaper. His heart lurched. The library book was not there.

It must have slipped out in the Ford Escort.

JOHNNY MASILELA

The workmen of Slovoville

OBLIVIOUS TO THE SCORCHING HEAT, the men of Slovoville had come dressed in jackets, and the women with blankets covering their shoulders – for that was the tradition, dating back to faraway tribal lands.

Now the men sat listening, their knees drawn up, some scratching in the hard ground with dry twigs. The women also sat listening, their legs stretched out in the dust. They all listened to Jeremiah Vimbi, the one of the ear lobes with large holes and an accent as rumbling as thunder. He was urging the people to think seriously about building a school for us, the children of Slovoville.

"One rand … two rand … no amount is too big or too small," Jeremiah Vimbi told the people while the hat went round. When it came back, almost everybody had dropped some money into it.

Then the people started deliberating on how the money would be used, putting their hands up for a turn to speak.

One voice from the crowd suggested that the money be used to purchase building material, "and red bricks as beautiful as the ones at the brick houses."

"The money we have collected will not be enough to pay for bricks," Jeremiah Vimbi warned the people.

"There is a factory that sells disused oil drums. With the money we can purchase the drums which we can then cut open and flatten into iron sheets. That way we can build even more classrooms," said Khoza, he from Malamulele, the land of the honey bee and mopani worms.

"But who is going to cut open the drums? Have you thought about that?" asked one parent.

At this point Grandfather raised his hand, and was allowed to speak. He cleared his throat and said: "I am surprised by the last speaker. If he really wants to know who is going to take charge of cutting open the drums the answer is simple: He and I and everyone of us here will have to do it. And, if I may ask, who else did the speaker think should do our own work for us? Back in my home village, the men dig graves with their own hands, not with white man's machines as you people do here in Slovoville. Didn't our forefathers teach us that any kind of work is possible with many hands working together?"

Another round of applause, and Jeremiah Vimbi had reason to smile.

And so a few days later work started on what was to be known as Jeremiah Vimbi Community School.

Disused oil drums, poles, not-so-crooked nails, wire, canvas and bags of cement were collected by members of the community for the building of our school.

Some of the material we collected from the place where the people living in the brick houses dumped their rubbish. They threw away valuable material, these rich people of the brick houses who called us squatters. We transported it to the site of the planned school in Jeremiah Vimbi's old truck.

On site, Grandfather and the other men chopped open with axes the oil drums, which were then flattened with five-pound hammers into iron sheets.

They straightened the crooked nails, all the time singing "Shosholoza", that beautiful song of men at work.

Then Khoza, the Shangaan from Malamulele, grabbed a sharp-pointed pick-axe to dig the ditch into which the poles were to be set up. Khoza lifted the instrument into the air, but alas! He missed the target, swearing in his native Shangaan as he did so.

Grandfather, he of the massive shoulders and hands that almost reached the knees, his shaven head gleaming from the sun, took the pick-axe from the swearing Khoza, and lifted the instrument into the air. The muscles on his neck and shoulders bulged.

Grandfather spun the wooden handle along with its pointed steel end into the empty air.

"Eu! Eu! Eu!" the women ululated while cooking for the workmen.

With the swift and rapid movement of a cobra, Grandfather spat into his palms, rubbed them together, and caught the pick-axe before it landed onto his head. Again the old man spun the instrument into the air, then raised both hands to catch the descending pointed end.

The women responded with shrills, while the men whistled in awe of such formidable agility and strength, and that in one of his age.

Grandfather, he who is reputed to have grabbed a puffadder by the tail before whipping its fangs against the stem of the mopani, lifted and held the pick-axe into position, heaved the pointed end into the hard ground and …

Shosholoooozaaaa … ooph!
Awuyeeee … ooph!
Kezo ntaaaabaaaa … ooph!
Is'timela sivel 'eSouth Africa …. ooph!
Wen' uyabaleeekaaaa … ooph!
Awuyeeee … ooph!

When Grandfather gasped for air and took a brief break, someone tried to shovel the fresh earth out of the ditch. Scoop! The shovel slipped from the man's numb and sweaty fingers, and landed with a light thud on his toenail, triggering giggles from us young boys.

Grandfather clicked his tongue in disgust, charged forward and snatched the shovel from the younger man.

Grandfather, he of the massive shoulders and hands that almost reached the knees, leaned the shovel against his leg, spat into his palms and rubbed them together. He grabbed the shovel with both hands, swung it backwards, stabbed the shiny blade into the fresh earth and …

Shosholoooozaaaa …
Scoop! Shove!
Awuyeeee …
Wen'uyabaleeeekaaaa …
Scoop! Shove!

Then the men heaved up the long poles and placed them upright into the ditch that Grandfather had dug. The poles were followed by rafters, and the rising structure began to look like the enormous skeleton of an animal believed to have lived long before King Shaka. The flattened sheets from the oil drums were lifted and heaved up to be dragged further up by men standing on creaking, self-made scaffolds.

They lifted their hammers in unison, these muscular men of Slovoville.

Shosholoooozaaaa …
Bang! Ooph!

At sunset the women gathered their utensils into bundles which they carried on their heads.

After washing their sweating bodies in the wheelbarrows, the men prepared to leave, leaving their tools behind. Jeremiah Vimbi, truckman and retired nightwatchman, would look after it. He had volunteered to stand guard overnight and had already arrived for duty, wearing an oversized helmet with a strap around the chin and a brown coat, just like the one Grandfather said was given to him after the war of Hitler.

The last of the workmen left Jeremiah Vimbi marching around the rising school building, truncheon under the armpit, a whistle hanging from a string around his neck. Chest out. Stomach in. Buttocks jutting out. Left, right. Left, right …

The next morning the men found Jeremiah Vimbi lying spread-eagled on the dusty ground, the silver whistle stuck in his mouth, and a stab wound in his chest.

The workmen's tools were missing.

Felicity Wood

The towers

THERE ARE THIRTEEN FLOORS below Jude and eight above her. There are three towers; she lives in the middle one. The towers are tall and cylindrical, and when the Southeaster comes roaring down the mountain or when the Northwester is howling up from the chilly winter bay, they sway, sometimes as much as three metres. Or so she's been told.

On her first day in the towers, she tried to open a window and the glass was nearly blown out. She hasn't tried opening windows since then, because the wind never seems to stop blowing. Also, she doesn't like getting too close to the window. The view makes her head spin: it drags her gaze down, down, down and then on and on and on. If she isn't careful and leans out too far, the wind and the view might pull her out.

The whole building encircles a central lift, encased in a well. The corridors go round and round; the rooms are all shaped like wedges from a cheese, the walls curving outwards. Jude longs for straight square walls, to be surrounded by shapes and surfaces that enclose her, that don't push outwards, into the void of roaring air.

She doesn't really know any of her neighbours. She works odd hours, sometimes at night, so it's not as if she's up and about when most other people are. Besides, the circular, windowless inner corridor is not a place she'd care to stop and chat; it gives her an uneasy feeling. She finds it a bit odd that she never hears any voices through the walls, though. But she suspects that many of the flats are like hers, small single spaces designed for single people who don't feel the need to be part of any sort of community, and just want somewhere cheap to stay near the city.

But one night she does meet someone. There is a noise outside, so she looks. A man, suspended in mid-air, is tapping on her window. If he were young and slender and fair, Jude might have mistaken him for an angel. But this man is stocky and dark, with the heaviness of middle age. His face is dragged into a strange shape by the wind. A bulky anorak flaps around him, and his feet, encased in heavy army boots, paddle madly in the air.

In spite of her state of shock and fright, Jude opens her window wide. The wind screams past, and takes the windowpane with it. She tries to speak, and fails. As she opens and closes her mouth at the man, he vanishes, a dark shape becoming one with the darkness. She leans out, so far that the wind snatches at her, her head spins, and her room starts tilting. Just in time she drags herself out of the wind's clutches before the tower can tip her out into the whirling blackness. But she doesn't see anything, nobody out there, nothing in the road far below. Is life in the towers driving her crazy? Jude wonders. Better not let anyone know about her visitor – just in case she really is going mad.

That night, she has bad dreams. The man's wind-distorted face keeps appearing in them, waking her up. Was he trying to harm her? Did she nearly fall out of her window because of him? The following day, there's a knock at the door. It's a large man in a heavy anorak, no longer frantically scrabbling for a foothold in space, but now shifting awkwardly from one foot to the other. His face still has a peculiar twist to it, perhaps now because he avoids looking directly at her.

"Good evening, Madam, could I have a moment of your time? I've come to tell you about our group –"

In mid-sentence, he thrusts a pamphlet at her. "This tells you where and when our meetings are. Perhaps you might care to join us on Wednesday evening at six."

"Yes ... but ... haven't we met before? What were you doing ..."

It is too late. The man is gone and Jude is left holding a poorly photocopied flyer. She squints suspiciously at it.

You are not prepared for what is about to happen in your life. Let us show you the way.

Heavens, no, Jude thinks, some loony religious group trying to take over my life. That man is bad news, and I don't want to find out why. Crossly she scrunches the pamphlet into a small ball, then drops it into the wastepaper basket.

Wednesday evening comes and goes. On Thursday night, there is a tap at her window. The man is back, tightly wrapped in his anorak against the gale. This time, he manages to grab hold of her window frame for a moment.

"You'll be sorry you didn't come to our meeting! Don't say we didn't warn you! But it's all there in the pamphlet if you want to find out what you missed!" he yells into the wind, before he's swept away.

142

Jude glares into the darkness. Then, against her better judgement, she fishes the pamphlet out of her wastepaper basket. It talks about letting go and surrendering oneself to the power that moves as the wind. Or is it the power that moves in the wind? She doesn't bother to re-read that bit, but skims on and comes across some obscure, vaguely biblical-sounding verses, hinting at something overwhelming, concealing more than they reveal. She finds the words unsettling, but she can't quite work out why. Until she reads what follows: *Don't think about escaping! If you try to hide from us, you'll find it's worse than letting go. You need us to help you face what's waiting for you!*

This is even nastier than a chain letter, Jude thinks. Who are these people? Why do they try to frighten me in this way? And how dare they pretend to know what's going on in my life? She drops the pamphlet back into the bin.

A few days later, walking down the curving corridor that leads to her flat in a state of mindless tiredness after a long night shift, Jude nearly bumps into someone, a skinny young woman with dishevelled hair and glazed eyes. The woman blocks her way, and grabs her arm with icy fingers.

"They've come for you," she whispers. "I know what's happening to you, because I live next door to you. But I won't let them get me, oh no. I keep my head down. I lock my windows and never open my curtains. And when the wind calls to me at night, I cover my ears."

"I don't know what you're on about. Please leave me alone!"

"Keep your voice down. They'll hear us talking. After all, there's hardly anyone in the building except us and them. They take everyone away."

"Who do you mean by 'they'?"

"Don't open your window, especially at night. I've heard them out there, calling to you. And I know what you're thinking too. Your thoughts are so loud at times that I can hear them through the wall. You're wondering why you hardly ever see anyone else here. That's because everyone vanishes, out into the wind. When new people like you arrive, they take you too. But I keep myself safe."

She rolls up a grubby cardigan sleeve and proudly displays needle marks on the bluish-white underside of her arm. Jude shudders. Then the woman flits, spectre-like, into the flat next door, leaving Jude standing, gaping, in the corridor. Well, there's one way of finding out if at least a bit of this is true, she thinks. She forces herself to start banging on doors, tensing as the sound of her knocking dies away. She knocks on one, two, three doors, but with no result. The fourth door, however, swings ajar immediately. The man at the door is familiar, as is his flat. It's just like Jude's, except it's completely bare, and the windows are flung wide open. There's no glass in the panes, she notices.

"Who are you? What do you want?" Jude demands.

For the first time, the man looks directly at her. His face still seems contorted, as if he's looking straight into the wind – or, Jude suddenly thinks, as if what he's about to say to her is causing him pain.

"Why did you listen to that woman instead of to us? Do you really want to end up like her? She builds a wall around herself with drugs, and she cowers behind locked doors. But we wanted to help you cope with what's going to happen to you. We're the messengers."

"What do you mean?"

"If you'd come to our meeting or even read our pamphlet properly, you'd have found out everything you need to know about what's in store for you. You can't get away from it – not unless you do yourself real damage, like that woman out there."

"I don't have to go along with any of this," Jude answers quickly. "I just want to get on with my life, and not be bothered by other people."

The man looks sad. "It's too late, Jude. You don't have a life. People who choose to stay in these towers usually have nothing inside, no real life of their own to keep them in place. They're so light and empty that the wind just sweeps them away. We wanted you to come to our meetings, so that we could prepare you for this, but we weren't able to. So goodbye, Jude. We won't be seeing each other again."

This is not real, thinks Jude. It's not happening at all. She backs out into the corridor. Get into the flat, she tells herself. Get out of this empty corridor, surrounded by rooms with no one in them. Find somewhere to hide.

When she opens the door to her flat, she finds the windows wide open, the place in disarray. The curtains are being dragged outwards. In a moment, it seems, they'll go careering off into wild vacant realms of boundless air. Close the windows, Jude tells herself urgently. Close the windows and the curtains and don't ever open them again. She stands in the window, fumbling with the catch and trying to grab onto the curtains. She stretches forward to get a better grip on them, but as she hangs out she feels the tower lean over, dropping her into the void. The wind grabs her and bears her with it, up and away. The towers and the city dwindle away behind her as she is borne across the bay, over the mountains, then on and on, and the wind sweeps all thoughts out of her mind, for ever and ever …

144

Dianne Ferrus

Going home

SHE LAUGHED AS SHE GREETED ME, holding out her cheek so that I could kiss her. I noticed that her grey hair was still uncombed – and it was almost noon already.

"Gosh," she said, while I walked slowly behind her into the kitchen. "I was expecting you tomorrow only." I noticed that the pots on the old kitchen cupboard had lost their shine.

My heart contracted as I looked at her more closely – the green floral dress was far too large and her seventy years were showing. Only her large black eyes still contained their old glint.

While I was unpacking my suitcase in the bedroom I heard her fiddle with the kettle. The unmade bed and the faded, drawn curtains disturbed me.

"How are you, Mommy?"

The wrinkled hand covered with brown spots held out a cup of coffee towards me and she turned around slowly: "The same. What's the use of complaining? Aunt Sara next door likes to complain – and you should see what she looks like." She laughed, her eyes two shiny slits. "But you know me – where I rule I do rule supreme and I never complain!"

We both laughed out loud and I looked at her again. This woman with an iron will, living alone in her four-roomed municipal house, how would I tell her? I shuddered, thinking of how she would react.

"And you, how are things in the Cape?"

"Okay."

My meek answer made her look up suddenly and her sharp nose pointed in my direction. Her eyes looked at me questioningly, but she didn't say anything. I couldn't ignore the frown on her face though, and I immediately knew that the magic was over for now. She felt it too. She knew I wasn't there for a casual visit.

"You must see what you can find to eat. Pinkie will be going to the shops only later. And don't expect to find anything nice; all I eat is a bit of jelly and custard and then I am full."

She was using the old tactics: as soon as she suspects that there is to be any talk about something difficult, she goes on the attack. The three of us knew this so well – my brother said that we should just leave her alone, she is old; but my sister and I felt that we were adults now and that it was high time that she treated us like adults and today it was my turn. Dad never had the opportunity before he died.

It felt as if I had been standing in front of the fridge for hours and still she didn't say anything to break the awkward silence. She just concentrated on washing the dishes in the sink – I could see that they hadn't been done for days. The fridge was almost empty. Instinctively my hand moved towards the bowl of custard, clearly off. I wanted to throw it away but instead I slammed the fridge door shut.

There was someone at the front door.

"I saw a car here, Carol!" Auntie Pinkie came to our rescue. "Hello, when did you arrive?"

I had heard that Auntie Pinkie was the only person Mom allowed into her house these days. She is a cousin of my father's and is just as old as Mom. Her dark face is always smiling but her large body is a burden to the ailing heart. She has been suffering from a heart complaint for many years.

"Hello, Auntie Pinkie. I came a short while ago. How are things with you and Uncle John?"

"No, don't ask me about that man, as long as he can drink, he is all right."

Mom and I laughed. Mom looked relaxed and asked Auntie Pinkie to light her a cigarette.

"You two are going to die from this poison." I couldn't let the opportunity slip by: "What does the doctor say about your lungs, Mom?"

"What can he say if there is nothing wrong with them?" But she didn't look at me.

"And Aunt Pinkie?" The two of them enjoyed teasing me, sitting there with broad smiles.

"Well, my child, I have been smoking all these years already. It's one of the last little pleasures I have left, what with your Uncle John's drinking ... I can come here to visit your Mom and then the two of us have a cigarette. I don't worry about it."

I wondered whether Aunt Pinkie knew that I knew about Mom. I had

146

heard it from her daughter Merna. I would have to speak to her on her own.

I went outside while the two of them sat in the front room, each with her own ashtray. It was a beautiful day in Worcester. The Brandwag Mountains were at their bluest. It was always like that in October. However, the peaceful day outside contrasted sharply with what was going on inside me. I knew that I would have to get it over and done with this weekend, whatever the consequences. Time was running out.

"Give her an ultimatum," Brian's voice had been impatient.

My mother couldn't bear Brian. And he kept blaming her for my unwillingness to marry him. Our relationship had reached a critical point. Brian thought that eight years was much too long for us to be stuck in a relationship. He wanted my final answer as soon as possible.

It was dusk when I went inside to wake up my mother on the sofa. She had fallen asleep there. She took two little sips of the soup I offered her and smiled. "Why didn't you wake me up?"

"Mom … I know about it."

She looked at me over the rim of the cup of soup and her smiled vanished.

"What?"

The loudness of her reply didn't frighten me.

"The fire last week … you could have died." Before she could say anything I silenced her with my hand. "You fell and were unconscious. I know everything. You won't let anybody into the house any more and you insult Aunt Sara. People borrow money from you and you don't get it back. You are forgetting people's names and you don't remember what you said." I spoke loud and fast. The knot in my stomach had disappeared.

I was ready for an angry response, but instead she sank further into herself and stared ahead of her, defeated.

"Why don't you fight?" I wanted to shout at her. "Don't just sit there – tell me that they are lying. Tell me that it was only a momentary lapse and that you will be all right again." But we both said nothing.

I sat down next to her on the sofa. She continued to stare ahead of her. The half-empty cup of soup stood cold on the dirty carpet.

And then it happened – suddenly the decision which I had been unable to take for eight years, which had hung over my head like the sword of Damocles, was so easy to take. I knew that I had to tell Brian that it was all over and that I would not be coming back. I had to tell him that the doctor had said that it was only a matter of months and that it wouldn't be getting any easier. Her brain was already affected. I was going to stay on. She was my mother after all and all I could do for her was be with her.

Some days were good, others were bad. But I discovered so much about her – the eyes that gleamed with joy when I read her my poems, and the ease with which she put her hand on mine when we talked to each other. When she was fine we dug the soil and planted whatever we could lay our hands on. I had really come home.

And then one warm summer evening in February she gently left. In the small garden in front of her flat the tomatoes we had so enjoyed planting in October, were bursting with red ripeness.

BRIDGET PITT

Ruby in the sky

RUBY LAY ON HER BACK, gazing at the wooden mobile turning in the wind. The row of coloured wood strips formed a seemingly endless spiral as they twisted up, and then down. These things could drive you mad, she reflected. Always moving, but never getting anywhere, like a rat on an exercise wheel. Phillip loved toys that caged movement. Like sliding orange blobs of oil trapped in illuminated bottles, or wooden beetles impotently waggling their magnetic legs inside walnut shells.

She raised herself on one elbow to look at him now, his thick lashes curled against a lightly freckled cheek. She liked watching him sleep. He seemed more predictable, safer, easier to love. Easier to feel that he loved her back. She felt faintly guilty, as if she were stealing something from him that he would not give willingly.

"Whatcha staring at, Ruby-in-the-dust?"

Ruby started. How did he know? His eyes weren't even open. He rolled onto his back, and appraised her through narrow shining slits under his lids. He stroked her cheek lazily with one curled finger.

"You'd better shake your body, girl. We're going kite flying today, remember."

Ruby flopped back. The kite was propped in the corner, shining purple and black through its cellophane wrapper. Phillip had bought it at the kite shop yesterday – a Jumbo Easy Flier, which resembled a psychedelic giant stingray, despite the friendly elephant suggested by its name.

"I had a kite when I was little," she said.

"That's cute," said Phillip. "Used to go kite flying with Dadsy, then, after church on Sundays?"

"No, he was too busy. Mr Mortimer took me. He was a friend of my folks."

"A friend of your folks! I say, how very kind. I bet he was one of those kiddy gropers. Did he stick his fingers in your panties? I bet he did. You probably encouraged him, you randy little bitch."

"Oh, gross me out!" Ruby giggled, although her laugh echoed hollowly in her ears and she realised that she did not find it funny at all. Phillip was smiling, but his expression was that of a cat toying with its prey.

"Well, never mind," he said, sitting up on the mattress, and stretching. "My dad never took me kite flying either. Yours was too busy brownnosing up the corporate ladder, and mine was too pissed, but bugger the lot of them. We'll take ourselves kite flying. Come on, woman!" He leant over and slapped her naked buttock, just hard enough to make it sting.

"What the hell are you wearing?" Phillip stared at her feet as she climbed into the rusty Golf beside him. "We're going kite flying, not mall cruising."

Ruby looked down. Below the knee, each leg was encased in smooth chocolate brown, ending in a wedge below her feet – three inches at the toe, rising to five at the heel. She stroked the leather, suppressing a smile as she remembered wearing them for the first time last week. She had floated along five inches above her usual height, feeling like a giant who could step over mountains, or like someone who could walk down the street in nothing but boots without a thought to other people.

She hunched her shoulders against Phillip's scorn. "I felt like wearing them," she muttered. "They make me feel good."

"Oh yeah? Well, you'll feel like a bloody polio victim trying to walk in those things on the sand dunes, I tell you that."

Phillip put *2Pacolypse Now* into the radio cassette, and turned up the volume. Ruby rested her head against the window. One blue eye stared moodily back at her from the side-view mirror. She let the numbing rhythms crash around her, blotting out thoughts and feelings. *They got me trapped* … moaned 2Pac. *Naw, they can't keep tha black man down,* contended the chorus.

Ruby tried to picture Mr Mortimer, but his features remained elusive. She could recall only the pale wrinkled hands that looked as if they had been left in the water too long, a small tuft of yellow brown hair nestling in a pink ear like a furry caterpillar in a flower, and a sense of suffocating embarrassment.

They pulled up at the dunes. Ruby trotted behind Phillip, her boots twisting and sinking into the sand. He walked fast, not looking back, whistling between his teeth. He climbed to the top of a dune, and sat gazing out over the sea, paying no attention to her laborious struggle up the slope. She flopped beside him, feeling sweaty and inelegant. Phillip leapt to his feet. "Come on, get your arse up. You can't fly a kite lying down. Hold it while I go over there. And don't let go until I tell you."

He began to run down the slope, and up the next one. Ruby held up the kite, gingerly – it felt strangely alive. The thin rods pressed through the material like the skeleton of an angular space-age bird and the tail flapped uneasily. The fabric slithered in her fingers, forming tiny rainbows of colour as it caught the sun. A sudden gust of wind tugged the kite out of her hands, and she watched it bump and fall down the slope.

"I didn't say let it go!" yelled Phillip. "You really are as thick as pigshit, Ruby. Can't you get anything right?"

They repeated the operation. This time Ruby held on until Phillip told her. The kite faltered for a second, skimming the ground, and then, as if making a sudden decision, swooped wildly up into the air. Phillip whooped with excitement. "Holy cow, look at that baby fly!" He flung his head back and crowed. Ruby grinned, longing to touch his throat and feel the unfettered delight reverberating in his voice. She squinted against the sun. The kite was a jewel in the sky, shimmering as it looped and dived at the end of the string.

She looked away, blinking at the green blobs burnt by the sun on her eyes. The wind blew a fine layer of sand, minutely reshaping the clean pale lines of the dunes. The dunes reminded her of Phillip's body, the same warm shifting planes and hollows, the silky gold sheen. It was beautiful up here, but pitiless, too. You had the feeling that if you died, the wind would just blow sand over your body, blow away your footsteps, blow away all traces of your existence. She shivered despite the sun, chilled by a sudden sense of desolation, the same feeling she sometimes had when gazing into the cool green depths of Phillip's eyes.

"Come down here, Rubicon!" Phillip called, his voice still alight with excitement. "Come hold it, it's orgasmic! Like holding the wind!"

She made her way down the slope, awkward in her boots. She knew she should take them off, but some stubbornness prevented her. She reached him at last, slipped her fingers through the plastic winder.

Phillip stood behind her, his breath on her neck, his warm hands over hers. "Hold it tight, baby. This kite is a tiger. Can you feel that? Bloody awesome, what d'you say?" He turned away. "I gotta take a leak. Just don't let go, whatever you do."

Ruby could feel the surge and tug of the kite running along the string into her arm. She was gripped by a strange blend of terror and elation that seemed to suck her breath away. The kite caught a sudden gust and dived wildly, almost touching the sand and then shooting skyward again. Watching it made her feel nauseous, as if she were being tossed into the air with it. She could feel its terror and hatred snaking down the line at her. She glanced around desperately for Phillip. He was standing whistling, his back to her, as he urinated over the side of the dune.

She looked up at the kite. Her arms ached from its tugging, the wind blew sand into her eyes. She glanced down, but instead of her boots sunk into the sand, she saw two small, white-socked feet bisected by the brown T of leather school shoes. Long brown Hush Puppies planted on either side of her shoes. She could feel the rough prickle of Mr Mortimer's serge trousers brushing against her bare legs, and smell stale tobacco overlaid with boiled cabbage and just a hint of egg. She felt a wave of violent nausea, and collapsed retching on the sand, frantically clawing the winder off her fingers and flinging it as far as she could.

"Holy shit!"

Phillip's howl jerked her out of her trance, and she glanced round. The kite was looping higher and higher, jerking the winder above the sand. Phillip ran past her, cursing as he snatched wildly at the line. He cut an absurd figure, his one hand fumbling at his open zip, the other grasping at the empty air. Ruby convulsed into hysterical giggles, drunk with the heady mixture of power and fear that comes when an object of worship suddenly mutates into a thing of mockery. She fell back and lay staring at the purple triangle receding rapidly into the sky, gasping for breath and heaving with silent laughter.

A shadow fell over her. Phillip stood staring down, his face thunderous.

"Fat bloody joke, hey Rubes?"

His voice was flat, unemotional. Ruby scrambled to her feet, trying to compose herself.

"I ... I'm sorry, Phillip. I didn't mean to ... I know it's awful ... but you looked so funny."

Phillip said nothing. Then he grasped both her wrists with one hand, and swung the other hard across her face. Ruby stumbled back, her face numb with pain, her shoulders shaking with sobs and hysterical laughter.

"It cost R350, you stupid little cow!" said Phillip. Without another word, he turned and strode off down the dune.

Ruby lay back, quiet now, feeling drained but strangely peaceful despite the throbbing in her cheek. The kite was barely visible – a tiny speck in a vast expanse of blue. She watched it until it disappeared behind the mountain. Then she sat up. Phillip was almost at the car. She could see the white-blonde cap of his hair bobbing through the Port Jackson bushes. They had both peroxided their hair a few weeks ago, but it looked better on him, she thought. It contrasted exotically with his dark eyebrows and olive skin. Her it just turned into a white mouse, with her light blue eyes and pale lashes. I think I'll dye it red, she decided. Ruby, the long pale paintbrush, dipped in scarlet.

Phillip was at the car now. He glanced back at her briefly, before leaping into the car and slamming the door. Ruby sat in the warm sunshine listening to the angry echoes of the engine as it revved down the hill. They were soon swallowed by a silence broken only by a faint twittering of birds and the soft whispering of the wind through the sand. She felt as if, like the kite, she were staring down on the world from an immense height, and nothing mattered at all. She carefully unzipped her boots, and, swinging them in one hand, bounded down the dune, relishing the warm grip of the sand as it embraced and released each bare foot in turn.

LUKE ALFRED was educated at the Universities of the Witwatersrand and Cape Town before becoming the then *Weekly Mail*'s unofficial London correspondent in the early nineties. In 1995, having returned to South Africa, he joined the *Sunday Independent* where he worked as a sports journalist and features writer, also for its sister paper, *The Saturday Star*, and *The Star* until his resignation in 2001. He now works as a freelance journalist and author. His first book, *Lifting the Covers – The Inside Story of South African Cricket*, was published by Spearhead early in 2001. He lives in Troyeville, Johannesburg, with his wife and three sons. "Dad's funeral" is an extract from Luke's recently completed first novel.

STIRRO MOFFAT BANDA was born in 1969 in Kagiso. He obtained A levels in World History, English Literature and Geography. Currently, Stirro works as a copywriter for an advertising agency in Johannesburg, and lives in Kagiso 2 with his wife and daughter. His home language is Zulu, but he speaks English, Swati, Sotho and other Southern African languages. He was inspired to start writing by the enjoyment he derived from reading Peter Abrahams, Chinua Achebe – and James Hadley Chase. Stirro has had a poem published in *Tribune* magazine, and he has illustrated a children's book, *Jamton Stories* by Jamton Cally Paynter, published early in 2001.

FRANÇOIS BLOEMHOF was born in Paarl, spent his childhood in various small towns, and studied at Stellenbosch University before settling down in Cape Town. He is the author of twenty-three books for adults, teens and young readers, and his work has won awards in all three categories. He has also published a large number of short stories in Afrikaans and English. His favourite food is pizza, swallowed down with a few Cokes. This means that he has to run and do sit-ups regularly. His recent work includes the controversial *Slinger-slinger,* which was one of the winners of the 1996 Sanlam Prize for Youth Literature, and *Hostis*, the first book, worldwide, to be published along with an original CD soundtrack, as well as a series of thrillers.

DANIEL BUGAN was born in Steenberg on the Cape Flats, where he still lives. At Spes Bona High, where he completed secondary school, his teachers encouraged his interest in writing and often read his compositions out aloud in class. After a brief period of studying Journalism, he now works for an insurance company and writes – in both Afrikaans and English – in his spare time. His short stories have been published in *You* magazine and in *Die stukke wat ons sny – Twintig nuwe Afrikaanse verhale*. He has written a play and is working on his first novel.

RREKGETSI CHIMELOANE was born in Diepkloof, Soweto, in 1964. After completing high school, he enrolled at a technikon, but his studies were disrupted by student unrest. He found employment as a maintenance operator in Sasolburg, where from 1986 to 1991 he stayed in a men's-only hostel. During this time he obtained a diploma in Creative Writing and joined the African Writers' Association. His first novel, *To be Like Siswe*, was published in 1992, followed by the autobiographical *The Hostel-Dwellers – a First-hand Account*, based on his own hostel experiences. *Whose Laetie are You? – My Soweto Boyhood*, was published by Kwela early in 2001. He lives in Soshanguve and works at SAB Rosslyn outside Pretoria.

Born in the Transkei, E.K.M. DIDO has lived in the Western Cape since 1972. She is the author of three novels, *Die storie van Monica Peters*, *Rugdraai en stilbly* and *'n Stringetjie blou krale*. She also writes short stories (one of which was anthologised in *Die stukke wat ons sny – Twintig nuwe Afrikaanse verhale*) and a literary column for the internet journal *LitNet*. After many years spent nursing and lecturing at a nursing college, Dido is nowadays working as a part-time consultant and full-time creative writer. She is particularly interested in the promotion of literacy and is committed to the establishment of a reading culture among all South Africans.

FATIMA DIKE was born in Langa, Cape Town, in 1948. "I am primarily a storyteller, then a writer, performer and poet," she says. Her professional career started at the Space Theatre in Cape Town, where she performed in the 1970s before leaving for the United States of America, where she lived from 1979 to 1983. She was one of the first black South African women to have plays published, with *Glasshouse* and *So What's New?* her best known work. Her plays have toured the world, and she has acted in many of them. Fatima has received the South African Women for Women Award in Toronto in 1997 and the Award for Outstanding Contribution to Literature at the 70th anniversary of Langa township. Her last play, *Streetwalking and Company*, opened at Cape Town's Baxter Theatre in 2000. She currently teaches Creative Writing at the New Africa Theatre Association in Cape Town.

TOM DREYER was born in Cape Town in 1972. He matriculated from Paul Roos in Stellenbosch, and studied at the Universities of Stellenbosch and Cape Town, obtaining an MA in Creative Writing. After lecturing in English at the University of Stellenbosch, he now works as a Java software developer. He is the author of two Afrikaans novels, *Erdvarkfontein* (1998), and *Stinkafrikaners* (2000), which was awarded the Eugène Marais Prize. His poetry was included in the 1997 *Nuwe stemme* anthology and in Gerrit Komrij's *Afrikaanse poësie in 'n duisend en een gedigte*. Tom has written for a number of publications, including *De Kat*, *Insig* and the *LitNet* internet journal, where he contributes i.a. photo-comics.

K. SELLO DUIKER, an advertising copywriter living in Johannesburg, was born in 1974. He grew up in Soweto and East London, and studied at Rhodes University, where he started a poetry society with a few friends. After graduating with majors in Journalism and Art History, he moved to Cape Town, where he completed a course in copywriting. His first novel, *Thirteen Cents*, was awarded the 2001 Commonwealth Writers Prize for Best First Book, Africa Region. A second novel, *The Quiet Violence of Dreams*, was published by Kwela Books early in 2001. Sello says that his mother, an insatiable reader, inspired his decision to become a writer.

DIANA FERRUS was born in Worcester in 1953. Although her studies at the University of the Western Cape were disrupted in 1973 due to the closure of the university, she has since completed a BA Honours and is completing a Masters in Women and Gender Studies, researching Black Afrikaans women writers. She writes poetry and short stories in both Afrikaans and English. Her work has been published in a number of journals and anthologised in *Taxi staanplek stories*, *Veertig is g'n vloekwoord nie*, *Women Writing to Create the Future*, *Die stukke wat ons sny – Twintig nuwe Afrikaanse verhale* and *Van oor die kontreie heen*. She is a founder member of Bush Poets, an all-women poets group, and of the Afrikaans Writers Association. Diana also co-ordinates the Women's Room, a weekly poetry jam at the Heartbeat Café in Lansdowne. She is working on her autobiography.

JEANNE GOOSEN is one of the most versatile – and controversial – authors in Afrikaans. She made her debut in 1971 with a collection of poetry, *'n Uil vlieg weg*, followed by *Orrelpunte*. Since then, she has become known also as playwright with a number of highly successful one-acters and cabaret texts to her name. But it is primarily as novelist that Jeanne has risen to prominence in Afrikaans literature, with *Om 'n mens na te boots*, *'n Kat in die sak*, *Louoond*, *Ons is nie almal so nie*, and *o.a. Daantjie Dromer*. She has also published short stories, in a collected entitled *'n Gelyke kans*. Her most recent novel, *Wie is Jan Hoender?* was published by Kwela in 2001. Jeanne's work is innovative and she is particularly well known for her wonderful sense of irony in her rendition of an often uncouth reality.

JENNY HOBBS was born in Durban, attended Natal schools, and holds a BA from the University of Natal, Pietermaritzburg. She worked as freelance journalist for more than twenty-five years, and her short stories have been published locally as well as overseas. She is the author of three novels, *Thoughts in a Makeshift Mortuary* (a finalist for the 1989 CNA Literary Award), *The Sweet-smelling Jasmine* (1993) and *The Telling of Angus Quain* (1997). Her other books include the teen novel *Video Games*, an anthology of quotations on books and reading called *Paper Prophets*, and the humorous *Pees and Queues – The Complete Loo Companion*, with Tim Couzens.

DIANNE HOFMEYR was born in Somerset West in the Western Cape. Her childhood next to the sea has been the source of many of her stories. She trained as an art teacher, and lived in Stellenbosch and Johannesburg before relocating to London, where she now lives and works as a freelance travel writer. Her novel *Boikie You Better Believe It* won the 1995 M-Net Award for Fiction and was broadcast on radio. Three of her other novels have also won awards: *When Whales Go Free, A Red Kite in a Pale Sky* and *Blue Train to the Moon*. Her most recent novel, *The Waterbearer*, is set against the backdrop of the fourteenth-century dhow trade along the East African coast.

ALLAN KOLSKI HORWITZ was born in Vryburg, Northern Cape, but spent his youth in Cape Town. He studied Literature and Philosophy at the University of Cape Town and has subsequently been involved in art, politics and education. His poems and stories have appeared in various South African anthologies and magazines. Allan, who lives in Johannesburg, is a member of the Botsotso collective. They publish books as well as a literary magazine and facilitate poetry performances.

BEVERLEY JANSEN is a poet and short-story writer living in Cape Town. She has worked as a teacher and as a radio presenter and still produces programmes for Workers' World Radio Productions on a part-time basis. Her work has been published in anthologies such as *Voices in a Garden, At the Rendezvous of Victory, iQabane, Optog, Protest Poetry* and *The Fate of Vultures* as well as in local literary journals. In 1996, she was selected as one of the Heinemann/BBC African Writers for her poem "The Surfer". She has also twice been awarded for her community work, as Western Cape Community Builder of the Year in 1999 and as one of 18 Community Builders of the Decade in 2000. In 1995, Beverley served as Fish Hoek's Mayor. She lives in Ocean View.

Born in Paarl, ELSA JOUBERT studied at the Universities of Stellenbosch and Cape Town, where she obtained an MA in Afrikaans and Dutch Literature. She started her career as a teacher before becoming a journalist, and has published seven travel books, eight novels, two collections of short stories and a collection of children's stories. She received numerous prestigious literary awards, including the Eugène Marais Prize, the CNA Prize, the W.A. Hofmeyr Prize and the Hertzog Prize. Many of her books have been translated and published overseas. Her best-selling and controversial novel, *Die swerfjare van Poppie Nongena*, was translated into thirteen languages and performed as theatre across the world. Her most recent books are the novel *Die reise van Isobelle* and *Gordel van smarag* about her travels in Indonesia. She lives in Cape Town.

GAVIN KRUGER was born in 1954 in Saldanha Bay on the West Coast, but spent most of his youth in Franschhoek. He studied Medicine at the University of Cape Town, and has his medical practice in Paarl, where he lives. His first novel, *Zink*, a winner in the Kwela, Engen & NNTV Writing Competition, was published in 1996. He also writes short stories, in both Afrikaans and English. His story "'n Troon vir Budd" was included in *Die stukke wat ons sny – Twintig nuwe Afrikaanse verhale*, which Kwela published in 1999.

MOSES SOVUMANI KAZIMKHONA MAHLANGu was born in 1974 at Klipgat, North West Province. He matriculated in 1992 at Bongumusa High School, in Phumula, Mpumalanga, and completed a BA and BA Honours (in Sociology) at Vista University. Moses started writing at the age of fourteen and has since published a collection of short stories and a drama and contributed to five poetry anthologies, all in Ndebele. His first short story in English, *The Past That Never Passed*, was published in the book titled *In Denial: Celebrating Youth Awakening*. He is currently working on an English novel and a non-fiction manuscript. Although Moses hopes to make a career of writing, he is at present employed as assistant lecturer in the Department of Sociology at the University of Pretoria, where he is completing a Masters degree.

JOHNNY MASILELA was born at the Holy Cross Mission Hospital outside Pretoria in 1957 and spent his childhood in the tobacco-farming region of Brits. He attended school in Warmbad, but dropped out in the turbulent mid-seventies. He worked as a journalist for the *Rand Daily Mail*, SAPA and the *Pretoria News* before becoming a full-time writer. He is the author of a novel, *Wisdom of the Ndebele,* and the autobiographical *Deliver Us From Evil – Scenes from a Rural Transvaal Upbringing*. An extract from this book was filmed as *Christmas with Granny*, which won the M-Net New Directions Award and the Manie van Rensburg Award for Excellence. His short stories were published in a collection, *A Place of Mud Huts*, and anthologised in *Crossing Over* and *At the Rendezvous of Victory*.

JAMES MATTHEWS was born in 1929 in a Bo-Kaap tenement building facing the city bowl. Today he is well known as a poet, fiction-writer and publisher. He is the author of a collection of short stories and four collections of poetry, and many of his stories have appeared in newspapers and magazines. Both his novels, *Darkened Windows, Darkened Rooms* and *The Party is Over*, appeared overseas in German and Swedish translations, while *The Party is Over* was also published locally in 1997. James's life and work was celebrated in *More than Brothers – Peter Clarke and James Matthews at 70*. In the 1970s he established the independent publishing house, Blac, and he still occasionally publishes books under the Realities Publishing imprint. He lives in Cape Town.

BRIDGET PITT was born in Zimbabwe in 1958. She grew up in Johannesburg and studied English and Psychology at the University of Cape Town. She has worked as a reporter on a community newspaper, cartoonist, high school teacher and editor, and has written for several educational publications. Her novel *Unbroken Wing* was published in 1998. Since then she has been writing life skills textbooks for Curriculum 2005. She lives in Hout Bay, Cape Town, with her husband, two children, two dogs and several fish.

THOMAS RAPAKGADI was born in 1969 in Alldays, in the Northern Province, and grew up in the countryside around Messina. He completed his primary schooling in Alldays and secondary education through Damelin College in Johannesburg. He has diplomas in writing, editing and public relations. Along with his siblings, Thomas worked on farms until the late 1980s, when he found a job as barman at a Pietersburg hotel. In 1991 he moved to Johannesburg, where he works as a security guard. He lives in Diepsloot township. His work has appeared in *Scope* magazine, and he is working on a novel.

ARJA SALAFRANCA was born in Málaga, Spain, in 1971 to a Spanish father and a South African mother. At the age of five she came to South Africa, where she has lived ever since. She holds a BA degree from the University of the Witwatersrand. In 1994, Arja received the Sanlam Literary Award for her poetry collection, *A Life Stripped of Illusions,* and again in 1999 for her short story, "Couple on the Beach". Her poetry has been published in journals, anthologies (i.a. *Like a House on Fire, The Heart in Exile)* and on the internet, while her short stories have appeared in a number of anthologies (*The Finishing Touch, LyfSpel/Body-Play, The Torn Veil).* A new collection of her poems, *The Fire in which we Burn,* was recently published. Arja has worked as a journalist for a number of years and is now sub-editor for the *Saturday Star* in Johannesburg.

BUNTU SIWISA was born in Pretoria in 1976, but he spent his first three years in Grahamstown, until his family moved to New Brighton, Port Elizabeth. He matriculated in 1993 from All Saints Senior College in Bisho, and then studied at the University of Natal, where he was a reporter for the student newspaper, *Dome.* After completing his MA degree in Economic History, Buntu was awarded a Rhodes scholarship, which took him to Oxford University, where he is reading for a DPhil in Politics. His short story, "Who Shoved Humpty Dumpty?", was selected for workshopping on *LitNet,* a literary journal on the internet, and another story, "Run, Afrika Run!", was published in *Icarus,* an Oxford literary magazine. He is completing a novel.

RITA SWANEPOEL was born in 1958 in Cape Town, where she still lives. She works for Telkom SA as a project manager. In her free time, she writes short stories and essays, a number of which was published in magazines such as *Insig*. Her novel, *Missis Victoria*, a winner in the Kwela Engen & NNTV Writing Competition, was published by Kwela Books in 1996. She takes a lively interest in local writing, and founded the Inkspot writers' circle in Bellville. Rita also serves on the board of the Afrikaanse Skrywersvereniging. She does volunteer work in the HIV/Aids field, and likes hiking and gardening for relaxation.

MARITA VAN DER VYVER was born in Cape Town. When, in 1975, she won a study bursary in a poetry competition, she enrolled for a BA and Honours in Journalism at the University of Stellenbosch. She later also completed a Masters degree on women in the Afrikaans press. After a year spent overseas, which included working as an *au pair* in France and washing dishes in London, Marita became a journalist. She also published novels for young people - *Van jou jas, Tien vir 'n vriend* and *Eenkantkind*. With her first novel for adults, *Griet skryf 'n sprokie*, Marita became an overnight sensation, widely featured in the media. The novel, a bestseller, won the ATKV Prize, the M-Net Prize and the Eugène Marais Prize and was translated across the world. Next followed *Dinge van 'n kind* and *Wegkomkans*. Marita currently lives in a small medieval town in Provence, France.

GEORGE WEIDEMAN was born in Cradock in 1947. When his first attempt at writing was published in his high school's annual, he knew that he wanted to be a writer. While still a student at the University of Pretoria, he had his first poetry collection published. This was followed by numerous collections of poetry, short stories and later also award-winning youth novels, like *Los my uit, paloekas!* and *Die optog van die aftjoppers*, which received both the Sanlam Prize for Youth Literature and the Scheepers Prize. His recent work includes the novel *Die onderskepper* and *Pella lê 'n kruistog vêr*, a selection from all his previously published poetry. His youth novel, *Dana se jaar duisend*, once again won the Sanlam Prize. His most recent book is the picaresque novel *Draaijakkals*, published in 1999. George lives in Cape Town.

MELVIN WHITEBOOI was born in Uitenhage, grew up in Port Elizabeth, and completed his schooling at Uitenhage High. He wrote his first short story, published in *Die Brandwag*, at the age of thirteen. During his term as fiction editor of *Die Burger Ekstra*, he wrote fourteen serials and developed the work of other writers from the Cape Flats for publication. From *Die Burger*, Melvin moved to *Rapport*, where he still works, as sub-editor. He has written several plays, including *Dit sal die blerrie dag wees!*, *Diekant, daai kant* and *Koffie en kondensmelk*, as well as radio and television scripts. He lives near Eerste River in the Western Cape.

 MARCEL WILLIAMS was born in Durban, where he completed his schooling before moving to the Cape to study Music at the University of Cape Town. After obtaining a teacher's diploma, he taught Music and English at secondary school level. He later obtained a BA, B Ed and M Ed through Unisa. He has always been interested in writing, but "finds it difficult". Since 1996, when he first started writing seriously, his work has been published in newspapers and in a book on art, *African Souces*. A previous version of "On a sunny day in Lavender Hill", called "Down in the hills", won the third place in the English Association's 1999 short story competition.

 FELICITY WOOD was born in 1961 in Cape Town and now lives in Hogsback in the Eastern Cape. She teaches English at the University of Fort Hare and is currently completing a Ph D thesis in English Literature. She is researching fantasy in comtemporary world literature and in local oral narratives, and is interested in how fantasy reflects aspects of traditional belief. Two of her favourite writers are Angela Carter and Ryszard Kapuscinski.

Word list

bakleiwyn – cheap wine, literally "fighting wine"
brak – mongrel or mutt
bra/ broer – "brother", friend
doek – headscarf
donner – hit
dorp – town
gaga – senile, insane
hak -(ed) – needle
heita – hallo, urban greeting
hola, hola – greeting
moja, wat sê? – what do you say to that?
hoenderhok – chicken coop
indod' omzi – the man of the house
kerksaal – church hall
klong – boy
lightie/ laaitie – child, youngster
lobola – brideswealth
mfowethu – greeting meaning "brother"
moer (-ed) – beat up, hit
moffie – homosexual, coward
nooit – never
ngwanake – my child
ou pel – my friend
ougat – cute
paddas – frogs
poep scared – "poop" scared, very scared (rude)
poppie – dolly
porzie – home
sharp, sharp – indicates agreement, answer to a greeting
snoek – Cape fish similar to pike
soutie – an Englishman

vastrap – here, standing firm
versterkdruppels – tonic, folk medicine
vlei – marsh
voetsek – go away (rude)
vreet hom – get him/ eat him
vrot – rotten
weh, nyana – salutation meaning "son"